Scared Angel

Oscar Farran-Ridge

Contents

1. Found

A man walks out of a coffee shop with a coffee in hand. He decides to walk into an ally which is a short cut to home. He happens to hear a tiny sob. He keeps walking not really caring much, until he hears a small wail which sounds like a baby. When he turns around he see a small figure huddled with a blanket in tattered clothes behind a trash bin. He approaches causing the small figure to sob louder. "I won't hurt you" He says walking closer and leaning down getting a better look. The girl is clearly older than he thought but he's not sure how much, he's thinking 18. The girl just cry's scared of the man but unable to say anything or run away. "I'm Aiden" he says after no response just cries, not wanting to just leave the girl there. She just looks up at him with big eyes when it starts raining, hard. Her cries turn into wails, Aiden stands and offers his hand to the girl not knowing what else to do. She hesitated before shakily taking the extended hand, just wanting out of the cold stinging rain. She's not fully able to hold herself up but he leads her to his apartment building anyway. The girl Seems to struggle to walk and leans on Aiden a lot throughout the short walk. This makes this taller man think the younger girl may be a little. As she is waddling and struggling with every step. She looks at him wearily as the man unlocks the door. She's lead into a living room that looks normal and she lets out a small sigh to be out of the stinging. Aiden closes and locks the door before taking his coat off. He looks at the girl wondering how to help her into new clothes since she isn't talking. "Would you like warmer clothes?" Hr asks the girl who is now laying on the floor on her stomach feeling the carpet. She looks up surprised by the voice, she lets out a grumble and goes back to playing with the carpet. Aiden decides to take control and since he has been a daddy dom in the past he decided this girl needed a bath. He picks the girl up and takes her to the bathroom. The girl lets out a scared breath and looks up with wide eyes. Aiden puts the girl down and starts running a bath. The girl not knowing what's happening she starts to cry. "This will make you feel better." The man says monotone before making the girl stand, which she does wobbly while sobbing. Aiden undresses the girl and puts her in the bathtub. She seems to struggle to sit up on her own with so much water but the man doesn't notice her nose go under water while she is trying to breath, sucking in water. She coughs uncontrollably so the man holds her up and forcibly washes her hair while she coughs. She finally gets a breath as the man washes the shampoo out of the girls hair which takes a few tries. He washes the girl clean which causes whines from her as tears continue to stream down her face. The girl is surely traumatized by this whole interaction.

He finally finishes and drains the water. He dries her and puts her in one of his t-shirts and a diaper he had from his past little. The girl squirms and kicks her legs scared of the man. He gets her padded and Carries her to the kitchen. He finds a protein shake and warms it up before putting it in a bottle.

The girl continues to sob as the man puts her down and warms the bottle. Once it is warm he walks over to the small figure and grabs her hand leading her to the living room. The girl trips into Aiden since she can't seem to move her legs that fast. He puts her in his lap a big roughly causing the girl to hiccup from fear. Aiden puts the tip of the bottle to her lips. Wearily she latches on after some help from the man. She hungrily suckles the bottle, gulping it down as fast as she could. Maybe a bit too fast. She's enjoying the substance so much she wails when the bottle goes dry. The man stands and burps the baby before taking her to the old nursery he had set up. The female doesn't stop wailing as the bottle only made her even more aware of her hunger. Aiden puts a paci in her mouth in an attempt to quit the sobs before placing the girl in a crib and closes the bars. "Goodnight little girl" he said before Turing a nightlight on and leaving the room. The whole night the house is filled with the young girls sobs. Sure she's out of the rain and off the street but now she's with a strange man and all alone in what feels like a box. The terrified girl curls into a ball and cries herself to sleep sucking the paci the man gave her, it helps control her hunger for now and she finally closes her eyes shaking from fear and the cold.

2. Penelope?

A/N : hi, I'm Rosie. I had this idea for a story and wanted to write it. If there's any mistakes feel free to correct me I'm not the best writer and I do have some learning disabilities. I have proof read for the most part but I'll need to read through again before I'm sure it's edited. I hope if you read this book that you enjoy and if you have any ideas I'd love to hear them. Thank you, xx Rosie

It's been a week since the man found the girl. He still hasn't learned her name and she's yet to speak.

She's even more terrified than the day he found her, she cowers every time he walks into the room. He scolds her for crying and punishes her for making any noises. He even screams at her to speak, like that would work. He even tried spankings which just made the girl more scared of the man.

The girl is currently huddled in a ball gripping her legs and trying to stay warm. The crib is bare except for a sheet on the mattress. Aiden walks in and she looks up with wide eyes. He's back, is all she can think. He walks to her and picks her up to change her diaper. He also puts her into a frilly dress. Once finished he puts the girl on his hip and carries her down to an already warmed bottle of a vanilla protein shake. He sits on the couch he lays her down on his lap before he puts the nipple of the bottle to her lips. At this the baby latches quickly, she's learned that the bottle is her only form of food since she's been with the man. The girl is too little to be able to escape the man and at times she knows she's better off. The man is scary though and her tummy is still always hungry after her bottles. The little girl cries when the bottle is taken from her. But of course, the man ignores her protests and grabby hands for the bottle. He puts her on his shoulder and burps the crying baby.

Once she lets out a few small burps Aiden picks her up and puts her in a car seat in the car. The girl doesn't know what to expect since she's never been in a car before. Aiden yells at the baby the whole way to the mall, he's mad that the girl never quiets her cries. He wants to get a few things for the girl considering the clothes from his past little are too big for the malnourished girl.

When the man comes around the car to get the girl he puts her on the ground making her fall to her knees and wail. He roughly picks her up and puts her in a shopping cart, luckily she fits but her knees are bleeding and the girl is a screaming mess. The man rubs his face with his hand and pushes the girl into the mall. He picks a few clothes before the girl points out a stuffed frog, Aiden didn't notice causing the girl to just reach and grab him. She's smiling for the first time since the man found the girl. When Aiden turns around he sees her big smile and he sighs. "If you stay quite I'll buy the animal" he says meanly. The girl didn't understand him except that he was mean, this scared her and caused her to whimper. "I'm serious" the man threatens, the girl hugs the frog close but manages to stay quiet with the new found comfort of the frog.

After what feels like hours to the girl, the man buys the clothes, diapers, and even the girls frog. When the man takes the frog from the girl to pay for it though this caused her to wail. "What did I say?" Aiden shouts causing the girl to hiccup as she sobs. At this moment a boy walks by, he decides that the man was mean to the girl. "Hey! Dats 'ot iice" he yells and walks up to the man as close as he can get. The man is much taller than the short little. Aiden laughs and pushes the boy without a word.

Penelope's pov : Im shopping with my sisters little, Linus. Im looking at dog toys "which one do you think Lars will like the best?" I ask as I turn holding up two dog toys....but I don't see Linus, I swear he was right behind me. 8 turn a few times making sure he's not down the aisle before I panic. "Linus?!?" I scream and drop the toys, Rushing around the store screaming his name. My sister is going to kill me, I think to myself when I hear Linus shout. I rush to the front of the store near the registers where I see Linus puffing his chest up against a strange man.

"Linus, come here" i sternly yell. He looks at me in fear, "aunty penny, this man is scaring this baby" Linus points to a girl who's clearly over 18 dressed as a baby in a shopping cart. When I look at the girls face she's has a look of terror on her face while making grabby hands at a toy frog. I assume her daddy just took the toy to pay for it. "Linus mind your own business, her daddy needs to pay for it" i explain as he runs to me and gives me a hug. The girl whimpers and my heart aches but I push the thought away, thinking I'm just jealous.

I've been looking for my own little for quite some time but I've yet to find the right little bundle of joy. Luckily my sister lets me babysit her little but it's not the same.

After Linus and I pick out a toy I take him to chick-fil-a and get him a kids meal. We're sitting in the food court eating when I hear a baby screaming like they're in pain. My mommy instincts look around and behind me I see the man from earlier. He is standing with the stuffed frog in his hand holding it over the trash can. His other hand is wrapped around the girls arm in a painful manner and she is reaching for the frog from the ground in sobs. I've yet to hear the girl speak but her sobs are enough of an indication that she is hurt and unhappy.

I rush to the man and snatch the frog from him, I had it to the little one before I pick her up. "Why would you treat your little like this?" I half yell in attempt to not startle the baby more. "What do you care? Besides she's not even my little I found her on the street, she doesn't even speak" he grunts before adding "you know what you can have her, I'm done" he walks away. The girl relaxes a tiny bit in my arms but then looks at me with wide eyes. It seems the girl knows I saved her but is still unaware of how to feel. She's clutching the stuffed frog to her chest. I carry the girl to where Linus is sat with our food. The girl is hiding in my chest when I sit down. She looks up at me curiously like a newborn baby would but then eyes the fries and nuggets in front of me. I wasn't the most hungry so I attempt to feed her a bite of fri. The girl is hesitant at first and closes her lips tightly but after the fri touches her lips I see her lick it with her small tongue. She slowly opens her mouth, her eyes widen and she starts to eat my food so quickly like she hasn't eaten in a long time. "Slow down munchkin" I try to sooth the girl. I'm not surprised when she doesn't slow but I let her eat until the food is gone. I feel glad that I tore the food into tiny bites so she wouldn't choke. "Woah aunty penny, she ate fast" Linus says with wide eyes and I nod in awe myself. I watch him look down at his left over fries and singular chicken nugget before offering them to the girl which she happily takes from him. I tear those up for her as hell and she happily munches. I wonder to myself if the man ever feed the poor girl. I think about what the man said, that he found her on the street. I think she needs shelter, I have an extra room so I decide I'm taking her home regardless of if she ever talks or not. I'm worried the girl is hurt and start to consider taking her to the hospital. It's at that moment the baby messes her diaper, I feel it on my lap fill up fast, she grunts and makes silly faces as she pushes, after a few minutes she relaxes for a Moment before she starts to cry. "Come on Linus, let's get the baby cleaned up and then back home" I say when I realize I have no diapers. I walk to the nearby diaper store to go buy a pack, luckily they have adult diapers. i also grab an adult frog paci for later that I'll put in my purse, just in case. I'm walking to the register when the baby makes grabby hands at a blanket with frogs and ducks on it. I can't help it and don't even think twice before I grab it and she snuggles close to it immediately. I smile happily and pay for the things, I give the girl the blankey before she can fuss. "Is this baby your new little?" Linus asks me. He's been pretty quite this trip and I think it's the confusion of the situation. "Well, I'm not sure Linus. I don't know what the baby wants or needs" I explain leading him to the bathroom with me. Luckily they have a family bathroom for us all to go into. I get her to the bathroom and lay her on the changing table. "I need to peepee" Linus shouts as if he just realized. "Okay Linus aunty is right here" I say. He's potty trained for the most part and just needs assistance when wiping. I go back to changing the girl. I admire her features for a moment. She is clearly over 18 but does look young. She is very lightweight for her age and doesn't even cause the baby changing table stress. She looks a bit sickly due to malnourish-ion. I change her into a clean diaper but when I pull her legs up she yelps and cries harder. I see dried blood on her knees and it seems something may be broken. I then see a rash so bad she's covered in blisters. It's that moment I decide she needs to get medical attention.

3. Eleanor and Frog

I arrive at the hospital with Linus behind me and the little one on my hip. She seems scared and like she won't come out of headspace, if that's even what this is. Linus on the other hand put his paci in his pocket and straightened up before taking a big breath. "Aunt penny, is she gonna be okay?" Linus asked looking spooked. He doesn't like hospitals and frankly neither do I. We sit for what feels like ages after talking to the nurse, when A different nurse calls us back. We follow the man in blue scrubs to a room with a 3 on it. We all scramble inside and the nurse takes some notes before leaving saying the doctor will be with us soon. I sigh and adjust the girl no my lap, whose been clinging to me like a monkey this whole time. 20 minutes go by before the door opens again. "Knock knock" the doctor says and opens the door. "I'm doctor Conner's. What seems to be the problem today" the doctor says while sliding his stool out and sitting down. "Well it's kind of a long story. This girl was in the mall today and got a Abandoned by a man who barely knew her. She was crying and screaming when she came with us to our table. She ate like she hasn't been feed in...i don't know how long.

And when she messed her diaper I had to change her, only seeing the worst rash I've ever seen, with blisters and blood. And when I went to bend her knees she wailed in pain. It seems she fell and her hands are bloody as well as her knees. I'm worried something might be broken." I shiver at the thought. "I also don't know her name or where she came from, doctor" Penelope finished feeling out of breath. "Alright so I'm gonna get some blood work, see if there's any trace of her in our database. I'm also gonna take a look at this rash and also just do an overall check of her to make sure she's healthy in every other area, then we'll have to wheel her off for an x-ray. okay?" The doctor is very caring and Penelope agrees. It takes 45 minutes for it all since the girl kicked and screamed when he tried to touch her. He even brought in a female doctor to help but it was no use. He finally got what he needed and excused himself saying a nurse will be in to take her to the X-ray room and that he'll be back with the results afterwards. Penelope sighs and leans against the hospital bed with a wailing girl in her arms. She rocks and bounces the girl only causing her to scream louder. It's then she realizes she left her frog in the car. "Linus, could you go get her frog?" she'd normally never ask but since he's out of headspace she can trust the 20 year old. He nodded and rushes to the car with Penelope's keys. Meanwhile, the nurse enters the hospital room to take the girl for her x-ray. She sees the wailing girl and coos "Oh how heartbreaking." "Is there any way I can come with?" I ask hoping they can pull some strings for the distressed girl. "I'm sorry ma'am but it won't be too long. Penny sighs and gets off the hospital bed, causing the girl to snap her head over to the woman she's been receiving comfort from with wide eyes. She reaches over and rubs her arm. "I'm be here waiting, buttercup" she tries to soothe but the girl doesn't understand and just reaches for the woman as she's wheeled outside. Linus comes back with the frog asking where the baby is. I explain as we sit and wait. It takes about 15 minutes before they hear the screams of the girl from down the hall. The woman leaves the room and makes it pretty far down the hall before spotting the girl. Penny runs to the girl and picks her up, the baby grips her shirt and sobs into her shoulder. The nurse pushes the empty bed into the room behind them. "The doctor will be in shortly with the results." Penelope just nods while comforting the girl. She hands the frog to her and gets the blanket out of her bag, and then sees the new paci she grabbed at the store. She walks to the sink to clean it quickly with warm water and dish soap. She makes sure the soap is gone before putting it to the girls mouth. The girl who thought it was a bottle opens her mouth. Although disappointed it's not milk she still happily lays her head on Penelope's shoulder. A few more minutes pass and Penelope is rocking the girl on the hospital bed when the doctor appears. He knocks and opens the door. "So I've got lots of information." He states while sitting in his chair. "This sweet girl, is Eleanor Rose Wilkins" he gestured to the girl. Penny and Linus take a moment to say hello to Eleanor. "She was abused by her parents and never grew older than 6 months. They never taught her a thing" the doctor sighs before continuing. "She's 23 now and I assume her parents left her to care for herself which she clearly cannot do. It doesn't mean shes not capable of growing mentally though, She's just quite behind for her age." The doctor adds. "She doesn't have a broken knee thankfully but it's definitely needs some bandaging. That rash is also pretty bad so I'm giving you some antibiotic rash cream. Lastly she's severely malnourished resulting in having low iron and other vitamins. I suggest getting her adjusted in a good meal plan and keep it consistent, as well as protein shakes, smoothies, and milkshakes are suggested." he stands and walks over with bandages. The girl stays in penny's lap and only cry's slightly from the bandages. Afterwards the doctor stands to shake penny's hand. "Do you have any more questions?" "Well I was wondering if there's anything I can do to help her with her weight that might work a bit faster?" Penny asks wearily. "Well since she's in a young mindset of an infant, you could always induce lactation but that's assuming you're going to care for her and if you're willing." He says and while penny had always wanted to breastfeed her little she knew this baby wasn't even hers and is afraid she may get attached. "Can you prescribe the lactation pills and I'll decide later?" She asks and the doctor nods. "That's no problem, anything else?" "No that's all thank you" she says. The doctor hands them the discharge papers and says they're good to go. So penny puts the baby on her hip and grabs Linus' hand thinking 'this is going to be a crazy week' as they head to the car.

4. Home?

OBJ It was a long trip home. Not because of the distance but due to Eleanor's upset screams the whole way. Linus tried to play with the girl in the seat next to him but she had no interest. "Aunty penny" Linus addresses starting to slip into a younger head-space. "Yes li?" I all but scream over the wails of the distressed girl. "Ewnor look non comfies" he states as simply as he can. I look back up through the mirror and see she's almost slumped and trying to hold herself up. She doesn't have the best mobility in her body. I don't know if it's due to the malnutrition and brutal bones or her lack of gross and fine motor skills. I finally pull up and help Linus out of the car, I can hear the screams of the 23 year old from outside of the car. I sigh and prepare myself for a whole new life as I open the car door and help her out of the car. I try to put her feet on the ground but she screams louder and clings to me. I lift her onto my hip and her crying subsides as she nuzzles into my neck sniffling heavily, I grab my bag and her few things as well as Linus sleep over bag since it's his night with me, while his mommy and daddy are on their date night. I walk into the room with her and realize I don't have any protein shakes for her. I let Lars, my Belgian malinois, outside to do his business and play. As I think of my plans for going to the grocery store and pharmacy I feel something wet on my breast. I jump and realize it's Eleanor's lips on my nipple through my shirt. I'm not wearing a bra and I almost pull her off but she whines in protest. I don't want to disturb her and the feeling is odd, but this is a clear sign she is still young enough mentally to breastfeed. With the new consent, I've decided if I'm going to care for the girl I'm going to do it right. Once Eleanor falls asleep still suckling, I pull her off and plop her paci in her mouth fast. I sigh when she only stirs a little before grabbing her blankie, draped around my shoulder, with her little fist tightening and loosening her grip ever so slightly in her sleep. I don't want to move her but I place her in the middle of the bed and put pillows around her body as well as her blankie and frog as well. I go online and search for a car seat in her size, the doctor told me she was five feet tall but only 72 pounds. I found one perfect for her size and ordered it. I watch the baby sleep next to me as I contemplate ordering a crib. I look at adult cribs but decide to build one like my sister and her husband did. I do buy an adult sized bouncer though for when I can't be by her side. Eleanor starts to stir and she lets out small coo like whines as she stretches I can't help but almost melt at the sight. I realize she needs some more clothes as she falls back to sleep. I end up making a large order of everything she may need before she wakes up. When she does open her eyes she cries and reaches for me. I smile and pick her up. "Did little Ellie sleep well?" I coo as she giggles and I pat her diaper realizing it's quite full.

• • • • • I let Lars back inside and got the baby changed before I helped Linus use the potty. I then got the kiddos strapped into the car once again. Eleanor didn't like leaving my arms one bit, and wanted us to know how upset she was by throwing everything we tried to give her for comfort while screaming loudly. I hope every car ride isn't like this, especially since Linus quite likes his car rides and tiny tunes with his aunty. I arrive at my local grocery store and get Linus and Ellie into a kids cart. I push the two around the store getting protein powder, vanilla breakfast carnations for Ellie's bottles until my milk comes in, I grab snacks for Linus that he points out and baby snacks for Ellie, I get some baby meals and baby food as well. Linus seems to keep Ellie happy for most of the trip until I'm waiting in line for our prescriptions she seemed to have had enough and wanted to be held. I didn't want to cause a scene so I pick her up as I walk to the counter. • • • Once back to the car Ellie is fast asleep. I'm grateful she fell asleep in my arms while waiting for the prescriptions to be filled. The pharmacist gave me a weird look but was kind enough to mind her own business. It took 15 minutes of waiting before I was able to strap the kids back into the car and drive us home. The car ride was peaceful with only the sound of a soft Disney song playing in the background as both kids slept in the back. I pull up at the house and sit in the garage while I order a pizza. After this day I don't feel like cooking, once it's ordered I get out and get Ellie first before I carry her around to Linus' side. I open his door "come on bubs we're home" i coo as I shake him awake. He opens his eyes and tries to push me away. "If you wanna sleep in the car and miss pizza then that's fine by me" I tease "you know aunty loves her pizza" I chuckle as his eyes widen and he quickly exits the car making a run for the door. "No running Linus" I scold while closing the door and walking inside. I put the groceries away while Linus plays with the toys he brought over. I heat up a breakfast carnation for Ellie and put it one of her bottles. The moment the nipple touches her lips she suckles hungrily as I feed her. I carry her to the couch and turn on octonauts for them. We finish our pizza while watching the childlike show, Linus eats messily in front of the tv while Ellie takes two small bites of my pizza. More like sucked on two small cut pieces and spit out the soggy crust. After a while Linus joins us on the couch, cuddling up with his Dino stuffy while sucking his paci and watching the show intently. Even Ellie, who is now sucking on her paci as well seems entranced by the tv universe. I smile down at the two snuggle bugs and pull them closer so they can both lay on my chest comfortably. I feel Lars jump up to snuggle into us as I give them both a delicate kiss to the head. We all drift off in each other's warm embrace.

5. First day

Penelope's pov:

I wake up to something wet touching my face. I groan loudly and roll over dramatically, when I do I feel something under me yelp before my hears start ringing. Out of surprise I inevitably rolled off the couch, causing me to look up. The thing under me? Eleanor... I jump up fast as she starts to scream louder somehow. I pick her up and put her into my lap "oh babygirl, I'm so sorry" I check to make sure I didn't hurt her and decide I must have scared her more that anything. I let out a sigh of relief, but instantly suck it back in. Where's Linus? And what woke me up that was wet? I look around and don't see any spills or evidence to where it might have come from. I see Lars sitting across from me and decide he was the culprit. I let him outside and fill his bowl for when he comes in. I suddenly hear a crash when I move to put Eleanor back down on the couch causing me to jerk my head towards to noises. 'What on earth is that boy up to?' I think as I March towards the sound of the crash. I hear soft cries coming from Ellie but clearly Linus is up to no good. I groan and search for any sign of destruction or the troublesome little. After what feels like ages I finally find that the tv in my bedroom has a hole like smash in it, as well as a baseball on the floor below it. "Linus? Are you hurt?" I call for him. I look under my bed and in the bathroom for him not seeing any sign of life. I huff when I hear a small sniffle, it was so quiet I almost didn't hear it. I walk towards my closet and open the door, I see little feet sticking out from behind my coats. "Linus, what happened?" He looks up with a startled look on his face. "I-I-I uz p'ayin' wid ball..." he stutters out and then bursts into tears "I 'owwy aunty penny" he wails and rushes to me wrapping his arms around my waist. I was sitting up on my legs as he held onto me and sobbed into my chest. I adjust the distraught boy in my arms so he lays across my lap. I rub his tummy. "I'm going to let your mommy punish you okay? How about for now we head to get breakfast." My sister has allowed me to punish Linus as needed but with Ellie in the next room probably still crying I can't focus on the matter. "Cakies?" "Okay cakies it is." I agree and stand helping the boy to his feet. He hold my hand as we walk back to the living room. Ellie is indeed still crying while hiccuping. I feel guilty as I pick the small girl up. She's only an infant and she thinks I hurt her and then abandoned her. I nuzzle her close and she presses her face into my neck suckling my neck as she try's to calm her cries. I turn the tv on to a Dino show Linus enjoys before walking to the kitchen. I need a high chair if I'm going to be caring for such a young minded bean. I carry the girl on my hip as I try to cook pancakes one handed. It wasn't easy but I manage to have a plate stacked with blueberry pancakes 15 minutes later. I plate Linus' cut up pancake on a Mickey Mouse sectional plate and give his a sliced banana as well. I plate food for myself before I mush up a banana in a bowl for Ellie and warm her a bottle. I put the plates on the table before I call out for Linus. "Breakkys ready, come and get it" i say in a sing song tone. I get Linus a sippy cup of orange juice and get myself a cup a coffee while Ellie sucks on my neck letting me know she's hungry. Linus comes pattering in and sits down after he finishes washing his hands. I sit next to him with Ellie in my lap. I go between feeding her bites of mushed banana and feeding myself. She makes a mess making me wish I had bibs for her, I make a mental note to order some. While I'm trying to clean Ellie's face I hear the door bell ring; causing me to stop wiping the squirming baby's face. "Mommy" Linus screams and goes to get the door. "Make sure it's mommy first" I make sure to warn him. I lay her across my body and take the top off her bottle. I check the temperature, making sure it's warm but not too hot before putting the nipple of the bottle to her lips and stand. I emerge from the kitchen seeing Linus run from the window and to the door unlocking it "mommy" he screams jumping into my sisters arms. I stand bottle feeding Ellie and smiling at the two. My sister couldn't have children of her own and looked for a little for a long time before she found Linus, I'm so happy they have each other now. "Hey Sheila, want a cup of coffee?" I ask eagerly. I don't get to spend time with my sister much but I enjoy spending time with her. "I'm sorry. Linus has a doctors appointment to get a new inhaler." Sheila frowns "but I'd love to come spend some time this weekend with you and this small little cutie." she finishes by tickling Ellie's socked foot causing an eruption of giggles from the baby behind the bottle. We both hear a hmph as Linus grabs onto his mommy's leg. He clearly doesn't want to go and after yesterday I don't blame the poor boy. I called Sheila last night during dinner and explained everything. I know she's going to have a tough time getting him in to see the doctor on time so I shoot her a sympathetic look as she picks the boy up and gives me a side hug. "I'll see you in a week" she promises me with a wave. Before the door closes I hear "wuv aunty penny" I chuckle and look down at Ellie, who has finished her bottle and is staring up at me. I burp her and help her into a warm bath. I thought it would be easy but the poor baby was distraught. I ended up in the bath with Eleanor as I got her clean. She turns her body into me and clings to my body. I rub her warm back making the water wash over her. I feel her move around and then latch onto my nipple again. I haven't produced milk or even taken the lactation pills yet but the doctor said dry nursing helps with the production of it regardless. I don't mind her doing it, who am I stop the girl from just needing some extra comfort. • • • After our bath I get us both dressed. Ellie has a toddler rice and veggie meal and I have some left over pizza and a salad. The rice ends up all over the floor and Ellie after I finish feeding her and myself. I clean her off and put her in her bouncer that came today. I clean up around the house while she watches dora. Even though it's only the first day it's gone by quite smoothly. I do start back work tomorrow as it's Monday but I work from home and imagine I can make time for my new priority. I walk back in to see the cutest sight, Ellie is sprawled out in the bouncer with a small blanket tucked around her. Her arms are strewn above her head as she grips her baby blankie close to her face and over her eyes. Her little feet are stretch out as she holds her frog tightly in her arms and her paci in her lips. I return some emails as she naps before I move on to read my book. I look at the time and stand to make us dinner. Deciding to make chicken and dumplings I just feed the girl the broth and chicken mostly. Once we're done eating and cleaned up I get a bottle ready for her and carry her to my bed. I get her changed into a fresh diaper and a cute onesie and me into sweats before climbing into bed and putting the bottle to her lips. She instantly latches and pickles contently as she flutters her eyes. I start to sing Vienna by billy Joel softly as she drifts. Once she falls asleep she leaves a third of her bottle. I put her paci into her mouth and pull her into my arms. I make sure my alarms are set before I drift into a peaceful sleep. I awake to screaming coming from beside me. Eleanor is rolled into the sheets and covered in sweat. The poor baby must have had a nightmare. I lift her up and she thrashes against me. "Shh shh it's okay I'm here lovely girl" I coo and caress her face. Her cries turn to hiccups so I stand with her and change the sheets. I get her into a clean diaper and decide to just put one of my shirts on her. We crawl back into bed and I lay her in my chest. She holds the hem of my shirt and pulls grunting. She spits her paci out and starts to cry when I pull my shirt up and help her latch to me. I start the lactation pills tomorrow so hopefully soon she will have all the milk her little heart desires. She settles down as she suckles, I can't help but fall asleep with her as she suckles me in her sleep.

6. Ouch

Penny's pov -

Letting myself fall asleep with Ellie attached to my breast was a bad idea. I woke up with my right nipple so sore since she was using me as a pacifier the remainder of the night. I switch my nipple for her paci as I put some chapstick on my breasts, it's the best I can do for now until I can get nipple balm. I sigh knowing I need to get ready for work. I'm a psychologist and hold tele-psych sessions online. I only go into the office once a week to file my notes from my clients and get any files I'll need for the following week. I take my first dose of medicine after I leave the sleeping girl in the bed surrounded by pillows so I can go Jump in the shower. Once out I brush my teeth and get dressed before drying my hair and doing light makeup. I pick the girl up gently and carry her to the kitchen while lightly rocking her. "Wake up Ellie bells" I tickle her tummy lightly resulting in a whine and cute stretch. I get her a bottle ready and myself some avocado toast with strawberries on the side. I give her small bites of the strawberries and then bottle feed her while I eat my toast. I finish with 10 minutes to my first appointment. I put the tv on doc mcstuffins earning the girls attention and let Lars outside. I leave my office door cracked so I can see her in her sleeper. I get my computer set up and sit down before I sigh, I miss her already.

~•~•~•~

Once half the day is done it's time for my lunch break. I actually have no appointments scheduled until 2:30 and it being just now 12 gives me just enough time to feed and put the baby down for a nap. Over the past 3 hours she's been an angel. I had 15 minutes between each session so I brought her different toys Linus had left each time to keep her happy. I gave her some baby puffs before my last session. She definitely loved the puffs, I check on my sweet Ellie and pick her up. She squeals and rubs her face into my chest making me chuckle. "Someone missed me." I tease and get her a bottle warmed as I make us some pesto pasta with peas, I make a salad for my side and toast a slice of French bread. Ellie gets sliced grapes and dry cheerios with her main dish. It's gotten easier to cook one handed. I sing nursery rhymes and dance in the kitchen with Ellie on my hip until it's ready. I put her in her high chair that came today causing her to erupt into screams. I get her a sippy and myself a cup of juice before I try to feed her but she refuses. I end up putting her in my lap and helping her drink her sippy of water. After her cries calm I get her to eat half of her plate and half her water before she turns her head. I get her bottle and see it's perfect temperature for her as I put it to her lips. She latched on softly and suckles slowly. I notice her sticking her hand through the buttons of my blouse and she grabs my left boob. I giggle since it tickles but let her drink up her bottle. Im so alighted she loves these protein shakes as they will help give her some lacking nutrients. Once she finishes she's passed out in my arms, I plop her paci into her mouth and carry her to the living room placing her in her sleeper, I strap her in and cover her with a small blanket and covering her eyes with her baby blankie. I check the time and see I have 30 minutes before my next session. Deciding to respond to emails in that time I sit at my desk and get to work. • • • I let out a very long groan once I shut my laptop for the day. Don't get me wrong, I love my job but caring for a little one on top of my very demanding job is something I'm still new too. I walk into the living room to see sweet Ellie laying awake batting at her toys that hang down from her sleeper. I coo at the sight before I can't take it anymore and rush to pick up the girl. I get her into a fresh diaper and lay on the couch with her on my chest. I'm enjoying the snuggles as I rub her back when I feel her try to latch onto my nipple through my shirt. I sigh and move my shirt and bra before I help her latch, I flinch at the still new feeling but know I need her help to get my milk to flow when it's ready. She seemed content to suckle on my dry nipple as it must have given her a lot of comfort last night. I end up falling asleep before Ellie finishes dry feeding. I don't think I was out long when I wake up to a painful feeling shoot up my breast and up my body. I yelp and sit up fast unlatching Ellie as she begins to cry. "Oh sweet girl, I didn't mean to scare you but don't bite me" I tell her as she looks at me confused. My comfort must have calmed her since she snuggles back into me. I hear a scratch at the door and let Lars back in, he sniffs Ellie causing her to giggle. "That's Lars, he's a doggy" i say in a childlike tone for her sake. I realize I was asleep for a almost an hour so I carry Ellie upstairs for a bath. She doesn't want me to place her in the water though when it's full and clings to me in the process. I get into the tub with her attached to me like a Koala. She isn't the most fond of me cleaning her body and hair as she grunts the entire time. Once she's all clean i get her out and lathered in lotion before a new diaper is placed on her. She squirms when I try to put clothes on her so she ends up in just a small t-shirt that doesn't even cover her diapered bum. She looks adorable, I coo and tickle her tummy lightly. She pushes me away but it's not a hard push. I stop and lift her back up "I'm such a meanie hm?" I chuckle and bounce her on my hip walking into the living room again. I put on Sofia the first for her and lay her on her tummy on the play mat with some toys. While I watch her figure out her baby toys I make a call to the closest Chinese restaurant. I buy myself some dumpling, orange chicken, lo main, as well as some chicken fried rice for Ellie. I sit in the floor and play with Ellie's 'pop up pals' toy. Her excitement and small claps when she presses the button and the animal pops up, bring me pure joy. Her butt goes back and forth as she lays still on her tummy. I try to help her sit up but she falls forward on her hands, I'm surprised she's unable to sit up correctly when I've seen her walk, although wobbly. I help her back to her tummy time position when the door bell rings. I get up to get the food making her cry loudly at my sudden absence. She reaches for me and scoots her body back and forth like she's trying to crawl but can't get the hang of it. "Hold on lovebug, I'm gonna be right back." I say rushing to the door. After accepting the food and paying, I close the door. It's that moment I look up to see Ellie walking very wobbly towards me before crashing down to the ground. It was almost like her little legs were going too fast for her body to keep up. Her cries become screams as I set the food down and run to her side. "Oh. It's okay baby" I coo and rock her. She eventually calms with my nipple being put in her mouth. I eat my food until she decides she's done and looks up at me. I'm mostly full so put her into my lap sitting up and feed her the fried rice. I regret feeding the young girl in the living room as I have a large mess of rice to clean up but she loved the rice so much she did a little dance between each bite. I love seeing her excitement for food but it's sad since it's due to trauma and being denied food. Once she's done and refuses more, I take her to her sleeper and vacuum the couch and floor. As expected, Lars my large Pitt bull/ Belgian malinois runs from the noise but unexpectedly Ellie screams and thrashes in her sleeper. I stop the machine once it's mostly clean and pick the girl up. She grips my shirt so hard her knuckles turn white as I rub her back. "I'm so sorry, buttercup" I bounce the baby and go make her a bottle. Once it's done I return ti the living room to see Lars eating the remainder of rice. I sit down and he curls up next to me laying his head on my feet, I adjust Ellie to lay across my chest and put the bottle to her lips. She latched on and drinks her milk fiercely, I don't believe it's from hunger but for the comfort. Ellie is asleep before the bottle is empty, I bring the girl to bed and place her down before I head off to get ready myself. I lay in bed and order more toys for the baby since she enjoyed her hide and seek pop up toy. I order some stackers, hard books, and lots of jingly things. I put my phone away and cuddle into my sweet girl. I can't sleep and after a few hours I decide to get up. I'm thinking of all the things that could go wrong. I am enjoying being a caregiver for the girl but I'm also afraid she doesn't want me as her mommy, she has no way to tell me otherwise. I sigh and get the wood together I'll need for the crib. My shed is always stocked and I love projects to keep me busy. I get half way through the cribs main build before I start getting tired. I walk to the kitchen and grab an apple to eat while I watch an episode of Dexter. Once the episode is over I stretch and yawn while checking the time. 3am...great I'm gonna have a wonderful work day tomorrow. I groan and walk to bed seeing how adorable Ellie is all sprawled out on my bed with her blankie and frog tucked in her arm. I crawl in with her, she must have sensed my presence cause she rolls over and smooshes into me. I giggle softly and nuzzle close to the sweet baby before drifting off to sleep quickly.

7. Two weeks later

Penelope's pov:

It's been two weeks since I started back to work. Elle isn't the most fond of it now as she just isn't entertained by her toys and tv the same she was when she got here. She seems to be in distress every time I leave the room. I've moved her play mat to my office floor where she does tummy time during my sessions but her coos and baby noises are heard sometimes causing a bit of an unprofessional atmosphere. I'm finished with my sessions for the day but I'm still sat at my desk getting some paperwork and emails done when I start hearing Ellie making a silly noises, I start to notice she's trying to mimics the sound of my mouse and keyboard. I chuckle while standing, it's definitely time for the work day to be over. I walk towards her and she squeals while reaching for me, babbling away. Once she's situated on my hip I walk to the living room. "Is that so? That must have been a crazy day" I pretend to know what Ellie is babbling on about causing her to giggle as I place her in her high chair. We've done a lot of practice over the last two weeks and she's finally able to sit in her high chair. We had eggs for breakfast and sandwiches for lunch which Ellie had extra small cut up bites of hers. She's still drinking her protein bottles as my milk is only dribbling out it's really not enough to sustain her. I'm currently searching through my pantry trying to decide on dinner as Ellie is slapping her high chair try and babbling on in baby talk. I decide to make myself some veggie soup hoping Ellie will like it. I get started and keep Ellie distracted by singing and dancing across the kitchen as I cook. She enjoys the wheels on the bus until dinner is finally done and I've got us each a bowl ready. I make sure to put some ice cubes in her soup and let it cool. I put some gold fish on her tray as I start eating my soup. Once it's cooled some I blow on her soup and begin spoon feeding her. She claps and bounces in her seat "yummy hmm, want more?" I ask while doing sign language for more and she nods happily and does the gesture back. Over the past few weeks we've been working on baby sign language so she can communicate with me better. She's gotten the hang of more but thank you not so much. She's sitting up on her own much better now and she hasn't tried to walk again since last time. Her doctor said she's going to mostly act about 6 months but due to her physical age being older she may catch on to older milestones sooner. I imagine she knows how to walk from being forced too but can't do it well on her own. We finish our soup and I get Ellie's out of the high chair and place her on the floor to get her bottle ready. She can't crawl yet but she has started to sit up on her own. She doesn't move much usually and just sits still while I warm her bottle but this time when I turn around with her bottle, she is half way standing while pulling herself up using the table. I drop the bottle onto the counter and grab her quickly "no ma'am you could get hurt" I lightly scold her tapping her hand with my finger before I carry her back to the bottle. It must be time to get baby proofing supplies, I think to myself as I sit down with her and adjust her to latch to her bottle. She sticks her hands into my bra and plays with my nipple, this has become a constant with bottle feeding. The more nursing we do the more she becomes infatuated with my breasts. The bottle becomes empty as Ellie continues to suckles the empty bottle. I reach over for her paci and replace her bottle. She whines but accepts it before she cuddles into me falling asleep shortly after. I put her in her sleeper and call to make an appointment for someone to come babyproof the house, we agree on tomorrow afternoon. I'm off and plan to have a good day with my baby while we wait for them to come.

• • •

I carry Ellie to bed once I tidy the house. I lay her on my chest once I'm comfy. I'm asleep fast but wake up before I know it to loud screaming. I look around frantically for Ellie only to find her on the floor, she must have fallen off in her sleep. This is all my fault considering I could have had the crib ready by now but was enjoying her cuddling too much at night and put it off. I sigh and rock the girl in my arms after checking for wounds. She tugs my shirt so I remove it, before I help her latch onto my boob and after a few minutes It feels different. I look down and she has milk flowing down her cheek. I gasp as she giggles up at me smiling wide "is it yummy milkies?" I coo wiping the milk off her face with my thumb. After a minute or two she runs out of milk and begins to whine, I switch her to my right breast. She latched quickly and after another minute she is drinking her new milk aggressively. "Such a little boob monster" I joke knowing she is already loving breastfeeding. She finally falls asleep about 30 minutes after she ran out of milk. Almost as if she had to make sure it was most definitely gone before she could relax enough. Once asleep I surround her with every pillow I have and head to the shed to finish her crib. It takes 4 hours before it's finish being built. I get the white paint and add the first coat. While it dries I check on the still sleeping baby curled up in the middle of the large bed. I walk down to the kitchen and make myself a cup of tea. Once my tea is empty I go back to the shed adding a second coat and then joining Ellie back In bed. ••••••>.<•••••• I wake up to a hand slapping me in the face followed by soft giggles. I squint my eyes open and chuckle at my baby sitting up staring at me with her hand up ready to smack me again. I grab her and pull her over my body. "Someone's feeling feisty this morning" I chuckle trying to get some morning cuddles but I feel her tiny head go under my shirt, that had risen up my body, and latch onto my breast. I jump a bit in surprise before I chuckle "not feisty, thirsty" I correct myself with a shake of the head. This girl is already so obsessed with mommy milk. I think about that for a moment, am I her mommy? I'd like to be but I can't decide that and neither can she really. I look down at her big innocent eyes staring up at me. She's gripping my shirt tightly and smiling at me. "Are you my babygirl?" I ask seriously knowing I won't get an answer. "I'd like to be your mama" I chuckle when the milk runs out and she unlatches with a pout. I switch her to the other side as she happily latched back on. Breakfast goes by smoothly. Ellie and I enjoyed some banana oatmeal, I have toast and coffee with mine though. Once she's cleaned up I sit on the couch holding Ellie while we watch doc mcstuffins. We stay like this for a few hours until the people come to baby proof the house. I instruct them on what to do as Ellie clings to me while shaking. I think men are spooky to her since the man who had her before me. I shiver at the thought and hold her protectively the whole time. Once they leave she is begging to nurse. I let her latch on, clearly not needing any help anymore. She falls asleep attached to my boob so I switch it for her paci while she sleeps. I lay her on my bed while I bring her new crib to her bedroom. I pick her up before placing her in her new bed. She stretches out and turns over in her sleep sucking her paci. I turn the baby monitor on that I bought with her mattress and walk out of her room leaving her to nap. I search for Lars finding him curled up on the couch. I take him outside to play catch with him for a while. We go inside tired from running. I get some water for myself and put ice cubes in lars' bowl. When I walk to the couch I find Lars already snuggled up. I turn the tv on and we cuddle in front of it; with me stretched out and lars laying his big body all across mine. This is how we remain waiting for Eleanor to wake up.

8. New Friend?

Penny's pov:

I wake up to my phone ringing, I groan and reach for it knocking it to the floor; I get up and get the phone answering as I sit back on the bed. "Hello?" I ask not having looked at the collar ID. "Bitch, where have you been?" I here my best friend screech. "I haven't heard from you in two weeks." I cringe realizing I've ignored her accidentally since I got Ellie. I end up explaining everything as I get up to make breakfast. "Can I meet her?" She squeals. I think about it for a moment, "well I think that should be okay, she might be scared and shy at first" I explain as I plate the small pancakes and fruit salad. "Yay! I'm on the way" she says and hangs up. I wasn't expecting it to be today...I shake my head at my crazy best friends antics and fix Ellie's bottles and myself a cup of coffee before I walk upstairs to wake the sleepy girl. When I walk in I see her sleeping with her butt in the air causing me to giggle. I walk to her and lift her out of her crib, she tries to push away from me and dive back into her crib. "Oh come on sleeping beauty! It's time to start our day" I sing song as she gives up trying to get back into bed but settles for pushing her face into my breasts. I rub her back and try to lay her on the changing table but she won't let me go trying to get to my boobs. "Someone wants my boobies first this morning huh?" I sigh, trying to give her a protein shake this morning instead of breastfeeding has already failed. I unbutton my shirt for her and she latched on immediately, I whence this time since she latched weird. Once I detach her and re-latch her correctly, she hums in contentment and closes her sweet little eyes. We nurse for a while until she finally decided she's done, I carry her to the changing table and quickly change her diaper and clothes into one of the onesie I ordered for her. Once she's dressed for the day, I place her on my hip and walk to the kitchen. She lays her head on my shoulder while I put the small pancakes without syrup on her high chair tray with her new sippy of water. I buckle her into her chair and sit to eat my own pancakes as I feed her some fruit in between bites of pancakes. She eats most of her breakfast only making a minimal mess. She won't touch her sippy cup and mostly spits the water I try to give her out. I read that 6 months olds struggle to get used to sippy cups so I'm not worried but I do need to try soft tip sippies instead while she's adjusting. I'm cleaning her hands and face when I hear my door unlock and then open. I hear Lars runs to the door and barks once before he sniffs Melinda, he runs between her legs to greet her like he likes to do. I pick up my unhappy baby and carry her on my hip to meet my best friends of 12 years. "Baby I've got someone for you to meet." I say in almost a questioning tone, the moment she sees Mel she hides in my chest and pushes as far into me as she can. "She's had a scary life" I tell Melinda sadly. She nods and sits at the far end of the couch as I sit on the other end. We talk about how our lives have been going and just everything else while Ellie is hiding. After 30 minutes she starts looking at Melinda through my arm but is trying to be sneaky about it. Melinda spots the silly girl and we make eye contact before chuckling. We go back to our conversation but after 10 minutes I start scooting closer to my friend. Ellie looks up at me but doesn't shy away like I thought. I watch the curious girl peak over at Melinda and reach up to touch her face. We both coo at her cute nature as Mel touches the girls hand on her cheek. "I'm Melinda, I heard your name is Eleanor" I hear my best friend say to her. "Your mama calls you Ellie so you can call me Melly, we have long names huh?" She asks as if she can understand her. Ellie just giggles and crawls to her lap. I smile happily at her accepting someone besides me, she makes sure to keep me in her sight the whole time but enjoys her talks with her new friend, Well Melinda talks while Ellie babbles. I enjoy watching the two for a little bit when my belly rumbles so I ask Melinda if she's hungry. She nods and asks for a cup of coffee, I smile and stand. She follows behind me with a still babbling Ellie. She sits at the kitchen table and Ellie watches me intently to make sure I don't leave her. Mel explains to Ellie everything I'm doing in great detail, which cracks Elle up. I start the coffee in the French press as I move on to make us a charcuterie board of snacks. I lay out Crackers of different kinds, mozzarella cheese, cheddar cheese, Brie cheese, pepperoni, salami, prosciutto, green olives, apples, strawberries, blueberries, cantaloupe and watermelon. I get us some stroopwafel cookies for our coffee and lay the board on the table before getting our coffees; making them to our liking with vanilla cream before sitting down with my cup and handing Melinda her own. We gossip about old friends while sipping from our cups. Ellie enjoys some fruit and cheese before she asks to nurse by basically shoving herself up my shirt. I notice the time and realize she could go down for a nap before lunch. I nurse Ellie while Melinda asks me questions about breastfeeding. "Does it hurt" I chuckle at her question. "It does but Ellie needs the nutrients." I explain. "What does it feel like?" I think for a moment before answering "well the sucking feels like a gentle tugging sensation, when done correctly. And the milk flowing is a tingling warm feeling. It's a feeling of relief when my breasts are full of milk." She nods and asks more questions until my breasts are empty and my girl is asleep. I stand to put her to bed, I put her paci in her mouth once she is in her crib along with her blankie. Grabbing the baby monitor, I make a quiet exit out of the room and back down to my friend. "Hey, mama" she jokes when I walk in. "Oh hush I'm not her mom" I sigh still very torn apart at the idea of if I can get attached in that way. "What are you talking about? She's an adult but she has no ability to care for herself. You said yourself that she had a scary life and she's so attached to you! Of course you're her mama! She may not be able to tell you with words but she sure does tell you with her actions." My best friends sucks in a big breath. "Are you sure?" I ask still insecure on the topic. She laughs and gets up to hug me. "Babe, I can tell that girl already loves you like any baby would a mother" she says this looking into my eyes and I can tell she really believes what she's telling me. "Hm, I guess your right." We go back to snacking and chatting and before we know it it's time for Mel to go back home to her man. She kisses my cheek and tells me she loves me. "And If you ghost me for almost a month ever again I'm gonna move in!" she screams as she walks outside and to her car. I shake my head as I close the front door and move to the couch before sinking down. Lars jumps up to lay on my lap licking my face and snuggling me. I decide it's almost time to wake Ellie but walk to make pasta in a creamy basil Parmesan sauce with sun dried tomatoes and garlic bread. Before the pasta is done I hear cries omit from the monitor. I set a timer on my phone for the pasta and run up to my distressed baby. "Hey hey, it's okay mama is here" I say to the crying girl. She clings to me covered in sweat, I begin to think she had a nightmare. She latched on through my shirt, shaking vigorously. She screams when I unlatch her to pull my shirt up but settles when my nipple comes to view. She suckles aggressively while I carry her down to the kitchen. I finish the pasta and carry her to her room for her to finish nursing in the rocking chair. She nurses as I rock back and forth soothingly, only calming once's she drains both my breasts. She looks up at me sucking my empty breast, it must have been one scary dream. "I'm sorry you had a bad dream pumpkin" I hum caressing her face gently. She unlatched and I help her burp before getting her changed into a new onesie and carrying her down to the kitchen. She clings to my front, laying her head on my chest. I sit at the table with her on my lap knowing she will be distraught if I detach her from my body. I got one bowl of pasta and eat some, after I take a few bites she turns her head to it and looks at it sideways.

I chuckle and put a singular pasta on my fork and let her try it. She mushes it between her teeth and smiles at me clapping her hands. Our lunch continues like this as I keep feeding her half of the bowl I fixed for us. The rest of the day is spent with Ellie doing tummy time in front of sesame street and then taking a nap on her play Matt with Lars laid next to her. I take a picture of the two cuddling and sit on the couch to return some emails. •••••••*•*••••••• It's dinner time and Ellie won't eat anything I made. I tried giving her bites of the grilled chicken, the steamed carrots, and the broccoli. She turned her head at everything. I warm up a protein shake in a bottle and try to feed her at least this but she refuses it as well. I can't let her not eat anything before bed but I also can't force her to eat. She cries and pulls my shirt and I finally give in and let her nurse. She drinks fast and hungrily making me frown. She nurses until my milk is gone and stares up at me with big eyes. I kiss her head and notice she feels a bit warm to the touch. I try not to over worry but I start to overthink. Ellie is asleep once again in my arms, I rock her for a bit before I place her paci in her mouth and lay her in her crib. I return to the kitchen and finish my dinner that's turned cold. I sigh while cleaning the dishes hoping Ellie isn't getting sick, she's still malnourished and is too susceptible to being hospitalized. I try to calm my worries while watching tv with Lars when I hear Ellie wailing from the baby monitor. I run to her side when I see the throw up beside her. I gasp and lift her up, she hiccups and whines, I get her undressed and go to change her diaper when I notice a rash all over her body. I instantly get worried and make quick work of getting her diaper changed. Her diaper was such a mess I decided to just take her to the bath, she wouldn't let me put her in alone so I join her. I get her clean before we exit the bath rather quickly, I lotion her as fast as possible so I can get her diapered before she makes another mess. I check her temperature and it's 100.1, I sigh and get her some Children's medicine to help reduce her fever. I decide against a new onesie and just wrap her in a blanket before bringing her to bed with me, she crawls onto my chest and lazily snakes her hand up my shirt to play with my right nipple, making milk beads out around it. I pull my shirt off and help her latch on as she sleepily drinks, falling asleep before it runs out. I replace my nipple with her paci but leave my shirt off. I decide since her onesie is off tonight she could use the extra comfort of skin to skin with me. Once the blanket is covering us both she moves slightly so she's covering my entire body with hers. I rub her back as I drift to sleep hoping my little one will feel better tomorrow.

9. Hospital visit

Penelope's pov:

I wake up to a tugging sensation on my chest radiating heat making it hard to breath. I look down and see that the heat was coming from my little one. Ellie is hot to the touch and whining while sucking, she notices I'm awake and unlatches to cry. She is letting me know she feels bad "oh poor baby" I coo. "I know you don't feel good huh?" Ellie doesn't understand me but cries more in discomfort. I go get a fever thermometer from the bathroom with her attached to the front of my body. I rub the thermometer across her head while Ellie continues her cries. It registers her temp, Reading 102.5, I groan knowing it's time to go to the hospital to be better safe than sorry. I change her into a clean diaper I had nearby in a cabinet of her things. I grab my phone checking the time, 3:34am wonderful. I put a shirt on hastily and then throw shoes on before I grab my bag. In this time Eleanor is in so much distress, she is flailing her limbs about while screaming loudly. "M...m...aaaaaa....mm...mmm" I here my baby babble clumsily before she lets out a loud shriek crying hard. "What is it my pretty baby?" I ask when I pick her up. She touches my face with both hands "mmmm....mmmmmmaaaaaammmm.... .aaaaa" she sputters out between cries causing me to gasp. I believe she might be trying so hard to say mama. "mama? I'm mama" I say happily with tears as I take Elle to her room. "Ma...ma" she finally says still crying but satisfied with herself she lays her head on my chest. Now that she's claimed me, I put her in a onesie much to her dismay as well as some leggings; she tried to fight me shaking her head and flailing her body but inevitably I won the battle due to us going into public. I get her diaper bag and some socks on her feet before I pick her up and make quick work to get to the car. I strap her into her car seat and get into the drivers seat before driving to the nearest hospital. She screams the entire way, I try to talk to her and sing but she doesn't calm. "Ma...maaaaaaa" she wails. "I know my baby, mommy is here." I try to soothe to no avail. It takes eight minutes for me to arrive at the hospital, eight long excruciatingly loud minutes. Hearing my baby scream for me when I can't hold her makes my eyes well up with tears but I have to be strong. Once I park I make my way around to my sweet baby and lift her into my arms I feel her grip my shirt immediately "m...mama" she sobs. Grabbing our bags before walking into the emergency room I walk to the front counters. I explain her state as well as her special case, the lady at the counter handed me a clipboard with paperwork. "Are you her legal guardian?" The lady asks me. "Well not exactly but she has no one else and I care for her." I say causing her to nod, "you should look into becoming her legal guardian, due to her special case she will need one." I take the paperwork and fill it out all while holding the still wailing child; she's stretching my shirt with her tight hold and it's now wet with tears and slobber as she is beginning to suck on my shirt in between cries. Once finished I bring the paperwork back to the desk and they call our name before I even have a chance to sit. A nurse comes to get us and bring us back to a hospital room. Ellie has moved onto sucking on my neck and it's that moment I realize I forgot her paci, frog, and blankie great! With Ellie's first word and my worries of her fever I left all comfort items behind aside from the ones attached to me, I roll my eyes at my forgetfulness. Once in the room I sit onto the hospital bed with Ellie against my chest still sucking my neck, surely causing a hickey mark but since she's calm I don't move her. I explain to the nurse her symptoms and they say they'll need to take some blood. I sigh knowing without her comfort items this is going to be dreadful. "Do you have any pacis? I know she's not an infant but her headspace is quite young and I forgot hers." I basically beg the nurse who nods "I'll see what I can do." It's twenty minutes before the nurse from before comes in with the lab cart. I don't notice at first but another nurse is trailing behind her. "I um have a little at home, and I bought this paci for him but has plenty your babygirl needs it more." the woman hands me the paci with a bear attached to it. "Oh my goodness thank you!" I smile as my baby latches on and is very entranced by the stuffy attachment. It's that moment the other nurse comes up and prepares the needle. I hold Eleanor close as she's still and playing with the tuft of hair on the bears head. The other nurse runs out of the room when the nurse cleans her arm and finds a vein "one...two...three, small pinch" the nurse injects the needle into Elle's vein causing an ear piercing shriek. Her paci has fallen and she tries to pull away but I keep her still. "You're doing so good my darling baby girl" I coo as she thrashes around, it's no use. She just looks at me helplessly while she tries to get away, as if to ask why I'm not helping her. "M...ama?" my baby let's out with her sobs, I wipe her tears with my thumb as I still am holding the squirming baby. The nurse finally removed the needle after getting 3 vials of blood. She puts a hello kitty bandaid on her arm followed by a bandage with pink bunnies on it. "Look at these little bunnies protecting your boo boo, you did so good my little one" I praise putting the paci she dropped when the needle entered her vein back between her lips. I see the door open when my baby has started to calm her squirms but has moved to bury herself as far into me as she possibly could. I look up to see the nurse from before walk in with a teddy bear in hand, "this is a gift from me to your little princess." She says handing my Ellie the bear and ruffling her hair before walking out with the other nurse. "Wow someone got extra special love hm?!" I coo and rub her back. She's gripping her new teddy tightly in her arms and she looks up at me sucking her paci when she spits it out and cries. "Oh darling what is it? You where just feeling better" I coo and pull her closer smooshing her face into my chest. She bites my boob making me yelp "no ma'am we do not bite" I scold waving my finger in her face." She looks at me sideways and pulls my shirt "mamamama" she grunts out while bouncing up and down, getting the idea I pull my shirt up and help her latch. "We don't bite just cause we want milkies" I sigh as she starts to relieve the all too familiar feeling of a full breast of milk. She nurses for 30 minutes before the door opens, not giving up the boob she just looks up at me as I cover her the best I can with my shirt. "Oh uh sorry about that ma'am" the doctor says while opening a near by cabinet and handing me a folded blanket "I can give you privacy if you'd like" he offers. Once I have the blanket covering us I respond. "No it's no problem" he turns and sits on his stool. "The tests have come back, the rash on her stomach is caused by scarlet fever, she should be fine after antibiotics, she also has strep throat, and an ear infection. I will be giving her a prescription of penicillin, she'll need to take the pill 4 times a day do you think she can swallow a pill?" The doctor asks and I shake my head knowing she couldn't. "Okay we will prescribe liquid, she will need to take it twice daily for 10 days and if her symptoms persist come back asap. You can give her childrens over the counter Tylenol or Motrin, and make sure to keep her hydrated." I nod and he leaves after making sure we have no more questions. I get our things and carry Elle to the car, I place ellie into her care seat making her whine. "Maaaaaama" she screams over and over. I'm grateful she's learning and that her first word was mama but her being sick is definitely causing her to use her new ability constantly. It's light outside and I'm hungry now so After picking up Ellie's prescription i drive to McDonald's. I get myself a McGriddle and hash browns before ordering a cup of apple and cinnamon oatmeal for Ellie. I look back at the baby that's emitting soft sounds before driving off, and see she's sucking your new paci sleepily whining and rubbing her eyes while hugging her new bear. Once home I get her into her high chair and feed her the oatmeal which she hungrily accepted all of while bouncing in her seat despite being sick the girl still loves her food. I eat my own meal before I carry her to the changing table to get the baby into a new diaper. I leave her leggings off much to her relief, I sit in the rocking chair and lift my shirt. Before my shirt hits the floor she's attached to my breast, I chuckle at the impatience and rub her back humming the song carry on my wayward son until her eyes finally droop closed. I put her frog paci in her mouth to sleep in and cover her eyes with her blankie. In her sleep she grip the blanket, I smile at the love she has for the soft cloth and grab the monitor before I leave the room and make it to my own, crashing onto my bed. All the exhaustion hits me at once and I fall asleep fast. ••••••••••••••••••

My sleep is short lived when only 2 hours later the monitor erupts in sounds all coming from my small girl. I groan from tiredness and sit up walking to Elle's room, "mamas here babygirl" i coo while lifting the girl up and laying her on the changing table. Once her diaper is off I see her reasons for screams, her diaper is all but overflowing. I get her mostly clean before I get a new diaper and cream on her and tape her up. I notice it's not lunch time yet so I get her medicine ready and help her drink it. She gags and looks at me betrayed. "I'm sorry lovebug" I coo before giving her a sippy cup, I've yet to find any soft tips since I haven't been to the store but I put apple juice mixed with water into one of the frog sippies I got for her. She just plays with it at first and tries to slam it to the ground. It takes some coaxing but she finally realizes this new toy of hers has a delicious drink inside to help rid her mouth of the yucky taste. I turn the tv to baby Einsteins and she crawls to my lap where I'm sitting on her play mat against the table. She lays across me holding her sippy lazily and staring at the tv, I notice she's mostly sucking air so I hold the cup upright for her earning a hum of approval. We stay like this untill lunch time, Elle is quite restless, being sick is going to make her nap even more than usual but also make it not as relaxing. I just cuddle her while she goes in and out of consciousness for the next 3 hours. When the clock turns one, I shift the girl to her stomach on the mat and go to make us lunch. I make some chicken and noodle soup to try and ease my babies throat and tummy. After lunch ellie is back to sleep. I put her in her crib for this nap, she barely ate her soup not really wanting anything but milk. The pharmacist did say that the antibiotics may upset her tummy. She ate a few noodles and spoonfuls of broth which is better than nothing before she pushed the spoon at me causing me to spill warm broth all over myself letting me know she was done. Her grouchy behavior indicates she isn't feeling well. I lift her up and bounce her as I put the food away. She lays her head on my shoulder and I hear her breath through her stuffy nose. I look over and see she's already asleep when I climb the stairs to take her to her room. •••••••••••••••• Soft whimpers wake me from the accidental nap I was having on the couch with Lars. By the time I'm fully awake her cries have turned to sobs, I rush to Eleanor's room to find her sitting straight up in her crib wailing loudly. Her whole face is red and snot and tears are running down her face. When Elle sees me she makes grabby hands towards me. This is the first I've seen her do this hand motion to me and I smile at her softly. "Still feel bad princess?" I ask as I lift her up into my arms. She's still burning hot as well as she's soaked her onesie with sweat. I carry her to the bathroom and run a bath, I make sure it's not as warm as usual but not cold either. I hope the steam and aroma therapy can clear her sinus and ease her scratchy throat a little. I undress us both and get her diaper off, she has quite the messy diaper confirming my idea that the antibiotics are making her tummy upset. She whines as I get her bum cleaned before I step into the bath, I hear her sigh and lay her head on my chest. I cup water over her back, grateful she's being soothed by the warm water. I feel her latch onto my breast as I continue to cup water over her body. Her suckles are slow and she doesn't seem to really care for the milk, just the comfort. We stay like this till the water runs cold causing Elle to whine. I get her lathered in lotion and diapered before she can make another mess, I then get her dressed in sleep pants with the character stitch from Lilo and stitch with a matching shirt. I lay onto my bed with the whimpering girl, putting her paci in her mouth causing her whimpers to calm some. Lars jumps up and paws at my leg before laying his head on Ellie's tummy and licking her face. Ellie giggles and puts her hand on his head and leaves it there, I smile at lars' added comfort and cuddle him as well by wrapping my other arm around him as I watch my little ones eyes flutter closed. We sleep for a few more hours until I move to make dinner. I bring Ellie to her sleeper and she doesn't move an inch meaning she must still be exhausted. I heat up the leftover chicken noodle soup hoping my baby will eat it this time around. •••••••••••••••••••• Ellie ate half a bowl of soup, I'm happy to get something into her tummy. She's nursed and is calmly sucking her paci while playing with the ends of my hair. I'm watching her as she looks up at me with sleepy eyes. "Mmm...ama" I hum and nod "I'm mama." I say with a smile, she smiles back and places her hand on my breast; and not even a second later her eyes flutter. I spend the rest of the night reading with my baby in my arms and Lars at my feet.

10. Rambunctious

Penelope's pov:

It's been three months since Ellie's been sick and she's much better now. She's zooming around the house on all fours, she's quite faster than me even on two feet. She's even progressed to say a few more words. She calls her sippy baba and her paci nee-nee. I'm not sure where it came from and It took me quite some time to realize what she was asking for but it it cute hearing her over the monitor when looking for her paci in her crib saying "oh...nee nee, oh...nee, nee neeeee." Currently I'm sitting in the living room on Ellie's play mat while she is slamming her sippy cup into it and I'm singing the itsy bitsy spider to her. She hasn't fully grasped her verbal skills but tries her best to sing along which is just sounds she thinks are the same as the words in the song. "Uh uh uh" she grunts moving her elbows and arms in a way similar to the chicken dance and bouncing on her bum; making me giggle and grab her up pulling her into my lap only getting more giggles from the girl. I smile down as she leans up grabbing my face, to give me a big open mouthed kiss to my nose. I wipe the slobber and kiss her nose back. She snuggles into me for a few minutes before patting my breast with her hand "want milkies?" I coo to my baby only earning hard tugs to my shirt. "Mamaaaa" She hasn't learned how to say milkies yet But we're trying. Elle drains my left breast before I move her to my right. I decide to turn some Disney tunes on, my little baby loves music. Her little bum starts trying to wiggle in my lap while still latched to my boob. She doesn't last much longer and she unlatches to wiggle her arms and legs in my lap. I grab her hands and I stand holding her up on her feet. She can't walk well on her own but she can stand up by herself. She steadies herself with my hold and continues to kick her legs out while shaking her little bum side to side. "Yeah Ellie! Go Ellie!" I cheer her on making her giggle. I throw her to the air and catch her, she shoved her face to my neck with a big smile on her face. I plant her feet back down to the floor holding her hands that are still wrapped around my finger. She's facing me now and she starts to do little squat like dances moving her bum up and down to the beat of 'I just can't wait to be king' from the lion king. My plans for the day are to take my lady bug toy shopping, she has necessities but just not enough toys in my opinion. She's more aware of her surrounding now and has grown quite the interest to the shows bubble guppies and Ni Hao, Kai-Lan which she calls bub gups and how how Lan Lan. She's now in her high chair slapping the tray with her hands singing "how how Lan Lan, saaa how how" over and over again. I'm thinking it's 'ni-hao Kai-Lan say Ni Hao'. I get the silly baby, a ravioli toddler meal ready in the microwave while; I get myself some left over chicken and dumplings for lunch. I blow her raviolis and feed her slowly. She makes quite the mess, luckily she has a lot of bibs in her collection to keep her clothes clean. I've gotten us dressed to go to the mall already so I'm trying to keep her adorable pink outfit clean. She finishes her meal and picks up her sippy. She loves juice now specifically apple, anything else is "bad juju" "Juju" I hear from behind me before I also hear a thud and then small bouncing. I turn to see Ellie's sippy on the ground, and Ellie's lip out in a pout. "Why'd you'd throw it, bug?" "Juju" is the only response I get. I pick up the empty cup and realize she is upset it's all gone. "All gone" I say before filling it back up with watered down juice and lift her up. I change her wet diaper before getting her blankie and tucking it in her arms. I clip her paci to her shirt as well as grab her diaper bag before my keys and lock up the house. I put Ellie in her car seat, she still doesn't love car rides so the moment she is in the seat her head slams back and she starts wailing. I put her sippy in her cup holder before closing her door and making my way to the drivers door. Once in the car I turn on happy toddler songs but when I look back her her screams have intensified. Her blankie is on the floor and so is her cup, I sigh and coo at her the whole drive. Once parked and out of the car I make my round to Ellie's door, her cries turn to sniffles when she finally touches me. She pull me as tightly as she can, I put her blankie and cup in her diaper bag before I sling it over my shoulder; making my way into the store. My coo's finally soothe the upset baby and by the time I walk into the toy store her eyes light up as she looks around in amazement. She lets me place her in a cart with a fun toy steering wheel attached, she pushes the middle button emitting a squeaky noise. Ellie continues to press the button throughout all the isles not giving me or the toys much attention. I ask her to look at toys I put in the cart but she doesn't look up until I shake a green frog rattle in front of her. She instant reaches up grabbing the packaged toy and shaking it vigorously giggling along. I smile and put a bear rattle in the cart as well. I'm looking at sensory toys when I feel eyes on me, I turn and look all around but I don't see any one in sight. My baby is still shaking her rattle happily so I just shake my head. I take a few steps away from Elle to look at a toy train when Ellie starts crying. I immediately turn to her and her rattle is on the ground and she's screaming. I let out a breath I didn't know I was holding, I thought something happened. I think while bending down to get the rattle and try to hand it to Ellie, she refuses though causing me confusion. I thought she was upset cause she dropped her toy, she's reaching for me. When I lift her out of the cart she clings to me as if she's scared. I push the cart to the register and all while paying I feel eyes on me. Ellie is crying softly into my shoulder as I walk us to the car and get our bags in before I get her strapped in. Separating her from my body causes her to scream "shh shh baby it's gonna be okay" I coo before rushing to the drivers seat and locking the door. I though we were safe but half way home I notice a black car has been following my every turn. I wanted to rush home and Ellie's screams make me want to get there faster, but this bad feeling makes me put her safety first. "I know you want mommy baby" I coo making quick turns going the complete opposite direction of home. After an hour and a half I finally lose the car, Ellie is still screaming and I feel my breast milk leaking from her hunger. She's overdue for milk and this whole situation has distressed her even more. I finally arrive home 30 minutes later and I rush inside letting Lars outside and crashing to the couch with my crying girl. I get my shirt off and she's latched drinking hard, She finishes quickly and whines for more. I switch her, and it's not until my left breast is mostly drained, when she finally relaxes in my arms. My milk runs out but she keeps suckling until her eyes fully drop and I switch my nipple for her paci. I finally relax myself rocking my sleeping baby in my arms. I sigh upset our evening got derailed, I was going to get us a pizza on the way home. I put Ellie in her sleeper with her blankie and let Lars in before I make myself a quick dinner. Ellie sniffles in her sleep but doesn't stir too much, I finish my dinner quickly and take Ellie to bed with me and lars. After today I want Ellie in bed with me, she nuzzles herself into my side once we settle into the mattress. I cover us up before Lars jumps up and lays across my stomach, I rub his head enjoying his comfort as I fall asleep with my little family.

11. Picnic in the park

Penelope's pov:

I'm getting Ellie ready for a day out with Linus. My sister called and she can't find anyone to watch Linus, when I said yes I could hear him over the phone begging to go to the park. Ellie doesn't want to be anywhere but my arms today though, making me feel uneasy at the idea. I reluctantly agreed so I take Ellie downstairs and get a picnic ready with snacks, peanut butter and jelly sandwiches, applesauce pouches, water for me, and juice for the kiddos. She's laying her head on my shoulder having just woken from a nap she's still a little sleepy. "Are you excited to go to the park baby?" I ask her softly after kissing her head. She just shakes her head causing me to frown in response. I was going to respond when the door bell rings causing Lars to bark. I zip up the bag with food before opening the door for my sister and Linus. "LARSYYYYYYY" Linus screams and runs to him. "I hate to just drop him and go but I'm running late for my appointment" she kisses my cheek and walks away. I shake my head at Sheila as she walks away She's always late "park park park!" Linus chants making Elle whine and turn into my chest.

"Babyyyyyy!!!!" Linus screams making Elle cry into my shoulder. "I'm sorry Li, she's still sleepy." I try to assure him but even I don't know if that's true. "why don't you go play while I give Ellie some milk." He looks to be thinking hard about my proposition before he nods saying "k" and running off, I chuckle and go to my bedroom to nurse Ellie. Linus' headspace is a bit older so he doesn't need breast-feeding, probably doesn't even know what it is. I get comfortable and lay Elle across my lap, she starts whining when she realizes she's about to get milk.

I'm half way through nursing when Linus burst through the door. Shit I meant to lock that "Aunty 'ook 'ook!" Linus screams showing me a paper with scribbles of different colors all over it. " waaait....wat yew doin'?" Linus asks with a tilt to his head. "Ellie is a tiny baby and needs milk from her mommy to grow big and strong like you." I try to explain. He scrunches his face up "mommy milkies?" he seems to be trying to understand, "...w-why can' I 'ot hab mommy milkies fom... myy mommyyy?" he whines in an almost cry. "Oh Bubs well are you a baby?" I ask him honestly. if he ever feels he could be in babyspace then we can talk to my sister together. Linus starts giggling "nuuuuu I big boy annn eben 'Otty trainededed" he says proudly. "I only need pullies at nitenite times." He nods big. "well you see mommy milk is only for little babies cause its not yummy to us." "soooo 'ot aste wike owberry milkies?" I chuckle "no not at all" he seems to have accepted that.

At this point w has finished nursing and is smiling up at Linus, defenently more awake now than before. "park?" I nod to Linus and pull my shirt up giving ellie her paci "neenee" she squeals. I smile wide at my lovely girl finally in a happier mood.

I get our picnic basket and Ellie's diaper bag as well. I usher Linus outside and lock up before buckling Ellie in her car seat and helping Linus get situated in the seat next to her. I turn on tiny tunes for them making Linus sing along. Ellie is softly crying in the seat trying to unbuckle herself, I frown wishing she didn't get so distraught in the car. Once at the park I get Ellie out and Linus unbuckles waiting for me to open his door for him. Linus jumps out giggling trying to run straight towards the play structure. "Wait wait" I say grabbing his hand. "Lunch first" I warn before getting our things. I lay the picnic blanket under a nice tree and hang Linus his sandwich and snacks. I get Ellie an applesauce pouch and feed it to her. Most of it ends up on her face and lap because she wouldn't stop dancing. "Mo mo" she pleads, I give her the last bit before helping her eat her sandwich and other goldfish. Once I get Linus and Ellie cleaned Linus runs to the slide and goes down a few times before climbing on the jungle gym. I decide to take Ellie to the swings and put her in the baby swing. She fits perfect but looks up at me with a quiver to her pout. "Shhh shh it's okay mommy is here" I coo and push her lightly, she begins to enjoy it and she swings for 30 minutes giggling her little head off. I hear a scream come from the slides, when I look up I see Linus throw sand into a little girls face. "One moment, pea.

Mommy will be right back" I assure her and walk to Linus, I hear her whine behind me but I'm focused on my nephew momentarily.

"What happened?" I ask as I approach the two. The little girl begins to spew tears and words only half making sense. I gather that the little girl wanted a turn on the slide and Linus wouldn't let her. She took a chance and went down after him causing this. "Linus that was very rude, apologize now!" I say sternly but hear Ellie's cry's grow louder.

"I-I'm sorry" he says not looking up from the ground. "Come on we're going home and your mommy will be punishing you for this one." He whines but nods his head. With his hand in mine I put my other hand on the girls back and lead the little one who couldn't have been older than nine to her mom or dad. I quickly explain what happened and apologized for Linus' behavior before I turn to walk to the swing set only to find it empty.

My eyes grow the size of saucers, she was just hear. I look all over hoping to find her near the set. I scramble all over the park and start screaming her name. "Baby goed?" Linus asks confused but I ignore him and run past the park into the woods surrounding it when a lady walks up to me. "What did your little one look like?" I stumble over my words explaining her outfit and basic features before she nods. "I got a weird feeling from a man walking around the track." The woman sucks in a big breath. "I noticed him walking into the woods with a girl of your daughters description. He...um got into a van with her."

I fall to my knees and sob, I feel Linus put his hand on my shoulder. "This is all my fault aunt penny" Linus cries falling next to me out of headspace. I can't say anything I just pull him to my lap. My baby is gone and who knows who has her. I can't believe I left her alone, I thought she'd be safe...I'm a horrible mother. My mind screams at me, before I push myself to I stand to my feet and call 911 to report a missing person. I hold Linus on our picnic blanket while gripping Ellie's stuffed frog and cry hysterically.

••••••••••••••

The cops come and make a report but warn me there's not much hope in the case. Once done I call my sister and head home, once we get home Sheila is already in the driveway. "She's gone." I sob in her arms, Sheila leads me to my house and takes my keys, unlocking the door and leading me to the couch. She covers me up and gives me a cup of tea. Linus and Shiela lay on the couch with me before I hear a knock to the door. I don't look up but Shiela comes and lets Mel inside. "Oh babe!" I hear before I feel her curl into me. I accept her comfort and lay my head on her shoulder. We sit like this for a few hours as I cry softly into my best friends shoulder until I fall asleep in her lap.

trigger warning

Eleanor's pov:

I'm crying again cause mama walked away. I miss mama, she is warm and nice. I suddenly feel a dark figure come up behind me. I start to scream for mama to come back when I feel something grab my mouth and lift me up. I'm squirming trying to get free but I'm throw into another man inside the go go machine. I'm screaming when I feel something cover my face and darkness overtakes me.

I wake up on a cold floor, my body starts to shake. Once my eyes adjust I notice the man who took me off the street. Tears start flowing from my eyes when I feel a slap to my face making me cry harder. I miss my mama, what if she no find me? "You think you can be a better baby for some bitch and not me?! I saved you, you little shit". I look up not understanding all his words but I shake my head no, not wanting to get hit again. I close my eyes and picture mommy while my eyes flutter from the incoming impact of the mean man's hand before darkness overtakes me once again.

A/N - I'm sorry, I promise things will get better eventually. I love you guys so much and I appreciate every vote and comment. If anyone has any suggestions feel free to message me or comment and your idea may make it into the story.

****Trigger warning****** Letting everyone know for the next few chapters Abuse: emotional and physical, grief, possibly other types of triggers. This is your warning. If any of these topics or similar topics are sensitive to you, please don't read these sensitive parts. Stay healthy and happy my dudes Xx

12. Not her legal guardian

A/N - List of triggers GriefStarvationName calling Physical violence(If I miss anything please let me know, it's never my intention to trigger anyone)

Third person pov:

Penelope had gone to the police station every day that week, she set up a search and rescue but the cops shut it down since after the park she was taken to a secondary location. "Most people never return from a secondary location, I'm sorry miss." The detective tries to warn me. "No! She is not gone" Penelope scream at the man. A detective not in the case observed the scene in front of her. Penelope see's the red head walk over and wave the man off. "I'm officer Parker" she says. Penelope looks into her sparking green eyes and almost forget why she's there, almost.

"M-my baby...sh-she's been kidnapped" the woman nods and gets Ellie's file "there's not much information here" the woman sighs before looking up, "is there anything you can tell me? Maybe anyone who might want to harm your daughter?"

I explain how I found Ellie and the man who had her before me. "He's a reasonable suspect" she nods her head while writing something down. "I'll review the camera at the park you took Eleanor to and see if he shows his face, if so we can look into our databases and see if there's any traces of him in our system." The detective explains to Penelope and she gets her hopes up. 'Maybe this warrior goddess can be the savior of my sweet darling baby.' Penelope thinks to herself but shakes the thought out of her head feeling guilty for the attraction she has for the woman.

"I'll call you when I have any details." Detective Parker says while standing and holding her hand out professionally. When Penelope reaches for her hand to shake it their eyes meet and they hold hands for a moment too long before they both break away. Penelope rushes out of the police station feeing a tingle in her belly.

••••••••••••••••••••

Once home Penelope is rushed with the feeling of emptiness. The laughter and happiness the girl once filled the home with his now vanished, even Lars is moping about the house.

Lars goes outside and comes back quickly to lay next to his human. He usually likes to play for a while outside but not since Ellie's been gone.

Penny knows she needs to eat but can't seem to make herself do anything. She hasn't even showered and has been wearing the same hoodie with stains on it, not caring about her appearance.

Penelope is angry at herself for not trying to become the girls legal guardian sooner, she just thought she had more time. The police say there's so much less she can do to help the girl. She's an adult but with her special case she needs a legal guardian to be able to make decisions for her. The police try to tell penny she ran away and is drunk somewhere but she's just a baby, not a 23 year old woman.

Penny groans at her thoughts and lars paws her hands before laying his body across her. "Thank you bubba" she sighs needing the deep pressure therapy he is giving.

••••••••••••••••••••••••

Ellie's pov:

I have no idea how long I've been away from mama. I don't think she's ever coming for me, the man who calls himself daddy is very mean to me. He won't give me food and only gives me a bottle a day, it's very yucky. He gave me a better bottle before I was with mama but now it makes me sicky in my diapiees that he keeps me in for long times. My bum bum hurts and I cry but he just yells at me but I just miss mamas milkies.

I also miss my oggy an an blankie an neenee. I start wailing and hear the door open, I open my eyes to see meanie daddy. "What are you being so annoying for, you little shit." His tone makes me cry harder, his pet names aren't nice like mamas were. I sob out "n-nee nee" I beg for any form of comfort from the man.

He laughs and kicks me over, standing on my chest and stomach making me throw up the white icky milk he gave me. Once I finish he slaps me hard, "you can't have anything. Especially not whatever a neenee is." I sob and try to sit up but he pushes me back down making my head hit the ground and the darkness wash over me.

Third person pov-

The girl is passed out with formula all over her body, Aiden walks out of the room laughing before he closes the door and locks it. He walks into the office with the rest of his gang. It's poker night and he's winning, which is why he went to Ellie's room to celebrate his victory.

When Ellie wakes up she crawls to the farthest corner, her head is pounding and she can't think as clearly as before. Ellie curls into a ball and uses her diaper again making her whine quietly due to her severe rash. This act overflows her diaper, leaving her in her own mess. She's shaking from being wet, cold, and scared. Her last thoughts before she lets sleep overtake her is 'I hope mama doesn't forget me.'

•••••••••••••••••

Penelope finally forced herself to eat, she had no energy to cook so just ordered some Chinese takeout. She's eating in silence when the door bell rings, she sighs before her and Lars go to investigate. She opens it to find her parents at the door, "mom? dad? What are you doing here?"

"Mel told us everything" her parents say stepping in and closing the door before they hug their daughter tightly. She melt into their arms and sob letting everything go, not needing to be strong for the time being. Her parents guide her to the couch and hold her for a long time before her dad goes to reheat her dinner for her. "Thanks mom and dad." Penelope sniffles. She wouldn't admit it but she needed to be cared for right now.

Penelope's parents know she struggles with depression and anxiety. During a time like this they knew she would try to be strong but her baby is missing and she needs them.

Her parents get their bags and move into the guest room, they plan to make sure she eats and takes care of herself starting with a shower.

13. Bolt the door

Triggers: Break down Anxiety Cuss wordsName calling Hitting Confinement Mention of a dead bodyStarvation

Penelope's pov:

My parents stayed for two weeks, my mom helped me shower and my dad cooked for me and helped out with Lars. As much as I appreciate their help and not being lonely, I was relieved when they left; I just want to be alone. My depression makes me feel solitary and I hate being social, even if it's just my parents.

Officer Parker called to tell me they found the man who took Eleanor in their database and he's on their wanted list. His name is Aiden Borden, it was a week ago when I heard from her. Ive been worrying myself sick thinking about who Ellie is around and what is happening to her.

Once my parents leave I get Lars into his vest and collar before we get into the car. I take him to the park where Ellie got taken; I don't expect to find her but being in the last place I saw her helps me feel closer to her, somehow. Once I park I help Lars out and we start jogging around the track.

He stops to pee a few times before we finish our way around the track, I take Lars to the car and get his retractable bowl pouring water for him into it before I drink my own water. When Lars is finished we hop into the car and I drive to a local coffee shop and go through the drive thru to get a cold brew and a pup cup for Lars.

When I get home I take a shower and eat a sandwich before cleaning up. I put all of Ellie's toys in her room, when I open the door my heart drops. I knew I wouldn't see her in there but seeing her room empty breaks my heart. I sit down in the rocking chair, I would sit in it to nurse Ellie to sleep and read her books. I start sobbing uncontrollably, I fall to my knees and scream in anger. "How could I let this happen to that poor helpless little princess." I blame myself.

Once I get it together I lay on the ground for a while before Lars come in whining for me to get up. I let him crawl into my lap licking my face. Once Lars helped me back onto my feet I take him outside and throw the ball for him, he only catches it a few times before he drops it and he's back to the sliding door whining to go inside, I sigh sadly he doesn't like seeing me so sad so it's making him sad too.

Lars and I are only cuddled on the couch for a few minutes before my door bell is ringing, Lars jumps up letting out a big bark. I stand and look into the peep hole seeing Officer Parker standing outside my door.

My heart start to pound in my chest, I silence Lars before I open the door and greet her with a kind smile. "I'm sorry to bother you." she says looking into my eyes sadly, it makes my heart beat even faster but this time due to worry. I shake my head and open my door wider for her to come inside. "can I get you anything?" I ask the red head walking into my living room, "I'll never turn down a coffee." she says with a smirk before her face turns serious again.

Once our coffees are made we sit at the kitchen table; we sit there in silence for what feel like ages before she speaks up. "my boss is making me close the case. I fought as hard as I could but it has been a week with no leads and...I'm sorry." She spews a bit unprofessionally but its not like I notice, my world just shattered. "I failed her" is all I can say before I break down again, I've been doing a lot of that today.

Officer Parker watches me silently for a few minutes before she stands and walks over, causing me to look up from my hands I was buried in. She squats to my level and smiles sadly before hugging me so tightly I felt I might break apart but then again it was as if she was making sure I didn't fall apart completely.

Third person pov:

Officer Parker stays for a long time, after comforting the woman she sits back down and distracts her from her grieving. They talk about how they grew up and where they went to college. Before they know it, it's midnight, the officer sends a small wave and goes to walk outside. "Oh, I'm Candice by the way." She introduces herself.

Penelope can't help but fall asleep dreaming of the red haired woman.

Penelope's pov:

I wake up the next morning to a call from my sister, she's been checking on me almost daily so I press ignore and roll over. Once I'm comfortable my phone rings again, I groan and grab it pressing answer. "You know you call me every day asking if I'm okay, we'll I'd be fine if you'd stop calling me and let me sleep." I say about to hang out when I hear her plead on the other end "wait wait please!" She sounds like she's in distress, I take a big breath. "What's wrong?" I regret instantly, I need you to watch Linus, PLEASE." I start to say no but she begs me again. "I-I guess he can come over." She thanks me a million times and says she'll be over in 15 making me want to cry.

I hope in the shower and brush my teeth before getting dressed and walking to the kitchen. After I get the coffee brewing I hear my door bell, I open the door and Linus runs straight to Lars giving him a big hug. I smile thinking this won't be so bad, my sisters steps in to my surprise and closes the door. She gives me a big hug and whisper son my ear "thank you so much for doing this, I know how hard it was to say yes." She kisses my cheek and gives Lars a pat on the head before kissing Linus "be good my baby boy" she says sternly before leaving.

I walk to the kitchen with Linus trailing behind me, I get him a bowl of cereal with light milk and make my coffee. I sit next to him while he eats his breakfast, he finishes rather quickly and asks for some juice. I get him a straw cup with apple juice hand it to him, when I sit down he looks at me weirdly before speaking. "Why Ellie's room gotsa lock on it?" He asks with a head tilt. I frown "well honey after that day in the park when she went missing, no one can find her." I tell him truthfully while a few tears fall. "Is she dead?"

That question, sent me over the edge. I didn't mean to scare Linus or scream at him but she can't be dead she just can't be! After a while of kneeling down on the kitchen floor I feel an arm touch my back, making me jump. "Aunt Penny I'm sorry" I hear Linus try to apologize but I can't respond, I'm too busy picturing Ellie's dead body. I hear Linus sigh and call my sister asking her to pick him up, she doesn't ask any questions though and he hangs up rather quickly.

It doesn't feel like long since I'm in the same position when I hear Lars bark, probably cause of the door bell I didn't hear. Linus let's his mommy in and she try's to hug me but I can't move. I faintly hear her tell Linus to go wait in the car.

Shiela is at the kitchen table leaning down with her hand on my back, she's been trying to get my attention for some time now but only this time so I hear her. "darling, come on let's go to bed." I hear my sister say lifting me to my feet. Once in my room, Sheila lays me down and covers me up before kissing my head. "I love you." She simply says and walks out, not long after I hear my front door close.

••••••••••••••

Ellie's pov:

I'm so thirsty and I want num nums, he never gives me num nums. My tummy hurts bad and I can't remember anything about mama just her pretty face, I don't remember what my neenee looks like though. I'm scared, I want to go to my home but daddy says I am home now.

I drink the bottle once it's brought in by the big man, he is always giving me my bottle and never speaks. Just sets it down and leaves, once the door closes I crawl to the bottle and suck it down hungrily, once half way gone I gag. It doesn't taste good but dada doesn't care,

I finish the bottle and crawl back to my corner. I wet my diaper that's half full and plop down whining at squishy feeling against my raw skin.

The door opens and in walks the man who gives my bottles but I haven't been to sleep yet so I know it's not bottle time. I watch him timidly as he walks over and takes my hand trying to lead me on my feet but I fall to my knees trying to keep up. He yanks me up making me cringe at the popping sounds my shoulders make, he swings me onto his hip marching angrily down a dark hall. He walks through a door and down another long hallway before he gets to another door. It goes on like this until he makes it to a double door, he gets key and unlocks it carrying me inside.

I cling to the man in fear and hide my face "oh poor baby" a condescending voice says. I don't have to look to know it's daddy, I while and nuzzle more into the man holding me, I haven't been held in a long time and I'm enjoying the comfort. "Look at me doll." I whine and look up making him smile evilly "Daddy has a surprise for you." He says ams walks down a short hall with a bunch of doors. He walks into one in the middle revealing a crib, a changing table, rocking chair, and dresser. I search for a comfort item but I don't see a stuffed animal or even a toy in sight, making me frown.

"What you don't like it?" Daddy screams taking me from from the man and throwing me to the floor. "Too bad you won't be leaving this room for a long time, ungrateful brat."

I can't help but just fall back slamming my head against the floor over and over as I scream and cry. I just want the nice lady back "maaaaamaaaa" I can't help but to cry. The door rattled indications it's being unlocked and then it's thrown open against the wall making me jump and whimper.

"Don't you ever call for that bitch again" he says angrily spitting into my face. "I am your daddy!"

He puts me in the crib and locks the bars connected from floor to ceiling. I whine but lay down happy to sleep on a mattress instead of the floor, before my eyes fully close I look for a blanket or something to hold but see nothing, I cry until my eyes drift closed.

I wake up to the man who calls himself daddy standing over me with a full bottle, I grab it instantly without thinking and put it into my mouth. I scrunch my nose at the taste but chug it down anyway, he watches me for some reason but I don't pay him any attention until he reaches down and takes the bottle making me grab the bars and pull myself to a standing position. "Nuu baba, back back" I whine reaching for it. Daddy slaps my hands making me cry, I fall to my butt as my tummy grumbles. My only nums....he just took it, my face slams down onto the crib mattress as I sob until my chest hurts making me sniffle. Daddy just laughed at me "you're still a hungry helpless little baby, huh?"

I sniffles as I eye him, he puts the diaper on the changing table before he grabs me. When he lays me on the table I try to reach for the baba but he scoots it out of my reach making me cry even harder. He changes my diaper making me scream when he wipes my owies, but when I scream his hand slams down onto my bum. I try to silence my cries but it causes me to start hyperventilating as I do. He puts a new diaper on me and then locks me back up, he throws me the remainder of my bottle before he leaves. I gulp it down as fast as possible while still crying, afraid he will come take it; my nums. Once finished I push myself into the corner of the crib and sob my little heart out.

14. Who are you?

A/N - a quick note to let everyone know that the pictures/outfits above do not belong to me. I do make the collages on 'ShopLook', that being said if there is a drawing or picture of a person it doesn't make it mine. Anyway I hope you enjoy

One year later

Ellie's pov:

I wake up in pain, flashes of last night flash into my mind and tears streams down my face like they did then. Dada hurt me again, he said I was a bad girl and I deserve it.

I stare at the bars and wish I had another life, one with a nice daddy. I sniffle, daddy doesn't like cry babies. I huff to myself and lay back down roughly falling back to sleep.

~Ellie's Dream~

There's a woman who looks familiar but I don't think I know her. "There's my sweet angel!" She says before picking me up and spinning me in a circle. I don't even know who she is but she makes me smile. I dream of her every night but this is the first dream she's talked to me. "Do you want to have some num nums with mommy?" The woman coos. mommy? I've never heard that word before but nod remembering num nums. I think there was a time daddy used to feed me nums. I don't remember him but I remember having a high chair, daddy says bad girls can't have nummies.

The woman who called herself mommy Carries me to the high chair I was thinking about that and sits me down opening a jar of food I stare sideways but when the spoon comes near my face I open up excitedly. The sweet taste over takes me and I open my mouth impatiently. "You like the banana, ladybug?" I nod my head and clap my hands "nana nana" I say wanting more.

~ ~ ~

I wake up with drool running down my face, I sit up and try to wipe my wet face but fail. I think about the woman in my sleepies, she was nice. I wish she was my daddy, or maybe it's...mommy?

I hear loud booms and shriek hiding in the corner of my crib. I hear shouting and banging noises for a while until my door opens. I look up to see a man I've never seen before he looks at me surprised and then turns outside the door "hey I've found a possible hostage, kidnapping situation."

When the man turn back he walks to me making me tense up as tears dolls down my face silently. "I'm not gonna hurt you." He says with his hands held in front of him, I don't know if I believe him, daddy told me that too but he always hurt me.

He walks out of the room momentarily and comes back with a key, he unlocks my crib making me shake in fear. He picks me up and cringes before looking down, "you poor thing" the man coos laying me on the changing table and changing my diaper. I cry out in pain when he wipes me, he gasps and puts a fresh diaper on me before carrying me outside.

It took a long time to make it to his car but when we did he buckles me in the back seat of a black car. I look around curiously not knowing where I am. I hear the man from before explain to a lady where he's taking me. When the man gets in the car he tells me he's taking me to someone he knows to fix my ouchies.

Penelope's pov:

I wake up and get started with my usually morning routine before I head to work. I've thrown myself into my work the past year, so I have a full day of sessions with clients.

I'm half way through when I get a call from Candice. "Hey I'm in the middle of work is this important?" I ask her. Ever since she came over a year ago and comforted me during my break down, we've been close friends.

"Cancel your sessions and meet me at the station!" She demands loudly. "Candice I can't jus-" "I'm serious, you'll thank me later" she assures me. I'm utterly confused and can't think of any reason she would need me to come there immediately....unless? No. I've pushed the thought of Ellie to the back of my mind, I have little hope I'll ever see her again.

It doesn't take long to arrive at the police station, oddly enough I see Candice waiting outside for me. "Hey, what's going on?" I ask getting nervous. She doesn't reply just grabs my arm a bit roughly and pulls me "where are you taking me?" I just get more confused.

She unlocks her car and gently pushes me into the passenger seat, "we're going to the hospital." She states and closes the door, my heart starts racing as she gets in the drivers seat. "Why?" I ask shakily. "They found Eleanor."

We get to the hospital and I run the front desk "Eleanor Rose Wilkins, can I see her?" I basically shout. "Are you a family or guardian?" Damnit. "No but I was caring for her before she got taken." "I'm sorry ma'am." Tears spill down my face as I tune the rest of what she says out and turn away from the desk.

Candice moves me aside carefully before going up to the front desk, I can't hear what they're saying as I focus on drying my tears. Candice waits impatiently for a few minutes before a man in scrubs walks out and talks to her.

The man walks over to me "listen Miss, I'm sorry but we can't bend the rules for everybody. She's in critical care and can't be seen by anyone but family. Have a nice day" he says and turns to walk away. I groan "wait!" He doesn't turn to me, tears spill over again but I don't stop them this time.

"You don't understand! This isn't a normal situation! She's stunted mentally and isn't like normal adults, please listen" I call out, he turns and walks to me. "I'm not her family but her family left her on the streets after abusing her. I cared for her before she got taken, please just let me see her?" I beg again making the doctor sigh. "Follow me." He says sternly before turning and walking fast but I'm right on his heels.

He leads me to a room with a number on the door. "She's pretty bruised and she has a few broken ribs. So far that's all we know that's wrong with her. She definitely has trauma from abuse." He says making my heart drop to my stomach. I was so excited to see my baby again, I didn't think of how much she could have changed over the year. "We still need to do a brain scan, she has possible brain trauma, if you notice anything worrisome buzz the nurses station." He informs before walking away.

I stand in front of the closed door for way longer than necessary just imagining the state she's in. I know I can just open the door and see her, but that's what I'm afraid of; is seeing her at her worst. I finally get up the courage and open her door slowly, I see the hospital bed and almost don't see her she's so small. Smaller than when I took her home, I let out a breath she's really here.

I move to a chair near her bed and watch her sleep not wanting to wake her but I can't seem to take my eyes off of her. I almost can't believe my own eyes when I see her own staring back at me. "Oh hi buttercup" I coo with a smile.

My head tilts to the side when she pushes as far away from me as possible. "Woo yew" she says pointing at me, my heart bursts into a million pieces. I want to cry but, I have to hold it together right now. "I'm mama, don't you remember me Ellie?" I ask as soft as possible but she just shakes her head. "Nu huwt" she whispers "I won't hurt you."I try to touch her hand but it only causes her to cry harder. "I'm so sorry, honey."

She looks up at me wearily "nu huwt?" She whispers again but this time in the form of a question. "I promise no hurt."

She lets me sit in the chair as long as I don't touch her. Some nurses eventually come to take her for a head scan. When they finally come back the nurses tell me she gave them hell, "she's a feisty one." I smile sadly. "Are you okay, Elle?" She looks at me and shakes her head no before she buries herself into the hospital blanket.

I mentally groan wishing I had brought her things but of course I didn't know I was coming here. I text Candice and ask her to come sit with Elle while I go grab a few things. She tells me she is on a case but that she'll send someone she trusts to watch over her.

By the time the cop arrives Ellie is asleep again, I stand and she takes my seat. "I won't be long" I say before rushing out and driving home as quickly as I can. I just hope she remembers her frog, paci, or her blankie maybe then she'll remember me.

15. Oggy and nee nee

Ellie's pov:

~~dream~~

I see the woman again and she looks like the lady by the hospital bed 'I wonder if I have met her before?' I think to myself as I watch her help me stand, I start to shiver because the mean men make me walk even though it hurts my legs; But she just holds be up by both my hands. We start moving our bodies in a wiggly way I don't quite understand but I'm giggling and the woman I met today is cheering me on. She's so nice, she deserves a good baby not a bad girl like me.

~~~~~~

Penelope's pov:

I woke up an hour ago and got coffee from the hospital cafeteria. I'm sitting next to Ellie's bed reading a book when she starts to stir in her sleep. I put the book aside and focus all my attention on her, she turns five minutes later and looks at me confused. "What is it, Ellie?" I wonder, she just shrugs and covers her head with the hospital blanket.
~~~~~~

"I have some of your things, baby!" I tell her hoping she will remember more if she sees them I pull out her comfort items. "NEE NEE" she shouts reaching for it making tears prick my eyes, I blink them away. "That's right sweetie it's nee nee" I agree putting the paci in the girls mouth making her smile.

All my stress and worry from the last year just washed away, seeing her smile made me feel a million times better. Even though she doesn't remember much and is afraid of me, she's safe and this is a big step to going in the right direction.

I reach down and grab Eleanor's blankie and frog when the doctor knocks briefly before he comes into the room. "Ellie did great through the night as well as this morning, she has a concussion and some brain trauma as well as her broken ribs so be easily lifting her. She will suffer from major headaches but I think she is ready to go home after lunch. Please work on her eating though as she doesn't seem to want anything without crying hysterically." I beam at Eleanor, "we get to go home, angel!" Ellie whines and hides her face in her blankie and frog, she seemed to have taken them from my hands while I was conversing with the doctor.

The doctor goes to get her discharge papers ready and I stand getting the bag together that I prepared for Ellie. While I'm putting diapers and wipes into her bag I hear a knock on her door before it opens slowly. I look up expecting to see a nurse but see my parents, Melinda, and Candice. "Hey guy's" I say confused why they're here.

Before they can respond a nurse comes in with a tray of food for Elle, she places it beside her before leaving quickly so my parents can speak. Out of the corner of my eye I see the girl scoot as far away from the food as possible.

"We know Ellie doesn't remember us but we brought her gifts." My mom says with a smile, I take the 4 bags and the heart shaped balloon and thank them. I put the gift bags with Ellie's bag and the shopping bag I have from the gift shop. I got her a frog stuffed animal but I don't want to overwhelm her, she barely remembers the things she already owned.

Ellie's pov: Im hiding under my blankie, I don't want to go back to the mean man, I wanna stay with the nice lady. I'm crying silently thinking about going back to the cold crib.

I peak out of my blanket when I see people come in with bags and a floaty thing, I want to poke it but I know they will yell at me.

I see them leave a few moments later, I pull the blanket off of me and look at the nice lady with a pout. She walks over to me making me flinch, she frowns stepping back and sits down instead. She reaches for the nums in front of me and tries to put it in my mouth, I put nee nee in instead and turn my body away Since I not allowed to have it.

She must have put the nums to the side cause I feel her slowly reach her hand out to rub my arm soothingly, I jump slightly at the contact but relax into her touch. She's so warm and it's making me yawn. 'I'm really sleepy.' I think sucking my nee nee and holding my blankie tight before I drift off.

Penelope's pov:

I watch as Elle falls to sleep quickly. The nurse comes in again shortly after to discharge her, I just lift her into my arms careful to not wake her before grabbing the bags. I get her to the car and buckle her into her car seat that I reinstalled when I went to get her things, I put the bags next to her and get in the drivers seat. I drive home as fast as possible trying to not give Ellie time to wake.

I'm successful and get Ellie into the house, I place the bags in the living room on the couch. Lars trots over and sniffs her wagging his tail and butt vigorously, I give him a pat before toting Eleanor to her room. I get Ellie into her crib and the monitor turned on before I'm out of her room and downstairs letting Lars outside.

Lars hasn't gotten any attention the last 2 days so we play ball for almost two hours, It starts to get dark when we head inside. I check on a still sleeping Ellie before deciding on spaghetti for dinner, it was one of Elle's favorites...before.

I get dinner started and hear Elle cry softly, it's only a second later before she is high pitched screaming. As I approached her door I hear "nuu nuu, nu wan be ere!" I open the door and Ellie hyperventilates "pea nu huwt." She begs, "darling baby I won't hurt you" I coo softly and walk slowly to her crib. She finally looks at me with wide eyes before reaching her arms out as far as they would extend and grabbing at the air.

"Nu go" she plees once in my arms. I bounce her on my hip "I won't go anywhere, mama is here" I assure her. It takes 45 minutes of rocking and cuddles before she fully stops her tears.

Dinner has been done for a while now but Elle wouldn't let go of me to let us eat at the time. Now that she's more calm I put her in her high chair and put a bib around her neck, she whines at me but doesn't cry. I think she doesn't have any tears left.

I try to feed her a bite but her eyes widen and tears well up in her eyes. No matter what I do, I try the airplane, boat, even the train in the tunnel with silly sounds didn't work. She turns her head with her lips sealed shut until I put the spoon away. I sigh as I get a bottle of formula but put vanilla protein powder in it before warming it in the bottle warmer.

I move Eleanor to the couch and lay her across my lap, I get the bottle near her mouth and she latched on sucking hard. I know she's starving and it breaks my heart she is so scared to eat, I have to find a way to help her eat again. When the bottle is empty she cries for more, I stand repeating the earlier process just thankful she's getting nutrition. Ellie only drinks half of the second bottle before she's looking around curiously, I have an idea.

I get Ellie's play mat and roll it out giving Elle her gifts to open. It takes coaxing but eventually she's tearing the paper excitedly. She opens a music toy, a stacking toy, soft books, another stuffed frog, and a stuffed pea pod stem toy.

Elle is enjoying unzipping and then zipping the pea pods, she even starts to unstack her stackers but stops halfway and crawls to the corner of the mat holding her new frog.

I don't want to push Elle, she needs to learn I won't hurt her on her own. I reach for the remote next to her making the poor baby flinch, I turn on 'team umi zoomies'. Elle stops shaking shortly after the theme song and becomes engrossed in the television.

I'm reading a book on the couch while Elle enjoys her show, I look up to see her butt in the air, her paci next to her while drool pools from her mouth, her little feet are sticking out from under her bum making me giggle. I take a picture and send it to my parents, Mel, and Candice as well as thank them for the gifts.

Ellie's pov: ~~dream~~

It's dark and I'm scared, I don't know where I am but I'm screaming loudly. Suddenly I feel pain erupt throughout my body as I hit the floor. The nice lady picks me up and rocks me. It didn't hurt too bad but it scared me a lot and the lady gives warm cuddles.

She sits in a chair and rocks me making me smile. Dream me tugs the nice lady's shirt causing her to remove it. I don't understand why I'm doing this but I watch as she pulls my mouth to the brown spot on her chest. I don't contest though and after a few minutes I feel my dream self relax completely . The lady looks down at me and I have milk flowing down my cheek but I don't care I just smile happily around her button. She makes a silly noise making me giggle up at her smiling wider "Is it yummy milkies?" She coos wiping the milk off my face with her thumb. After a minute or two the milk stops, I feel sad as dream me starts to whine, but the nice lady just switches me to her other side where I come face to face with another brown button. I wrap my mouth greedily around the button wanting the milk quickly and after another minute more milk is flowing; I drink this new milk aggressively. "Such a little boob monster" she giggles as my eyes close in contentment.

16. Soapy water

Penelope's pov:

I wake up late the next day, Elle slept in her crib soundly after I moved her until around midnight when she woke up crying periodically. She finally stayed asleep after seven am, it's now almost noon so I stretch and yawn waking up fully. After a warm shower I make some small pancakes and cut up some fruit, hoping to get Ellie to eat some today. I called my doctor and phoned in new lactation pills, I have no idea if Ellie even wants to breastfeed from me but I want her to have the option if the situation arises.

I lift the sleepy girl from her crib getting her changed into a fresh diaper before she's even awake. I coo as her eyes start opening "there's my little angel." She looks up at me but doesn't cry which is a good sign, she does push her head into my chest making me smile. Although it causes Whine's to emit from the small girl when I put her in the high chair but quiets down when I sit in front of her with a plate of pancakes and fruit.

"Alright babygirl let's try to have some num nums okay?" She looks wearily at me but seems to brighten up a bit when I say 'num num' she doesn't open up immediately but I'm very determined today. "Come on, pea. It's yummy see." I say before making a big show of taking a bite of a pancake "om num num! So yummy" I say extra enthusiastically. She eyes me with a look I can't place, I try the train in the tunnel trick and put the spoon near her lips again expecting another turn. She looks into my eyes before slowly opening her mouth, she didn't open wide enough for the spoon but enough for me to lightly push it into her mouth. Once the strawberry is in her mouth she beings bouncing but stops and looks at me almost as if waiting for me to scold her. "You did so good baby!!" I praise. I give her another bite making her happy dances return, this continues for a little bit. Her bites are small and she barely gets even half of the plate down, but I'm so proud of her anyway.

I lift her up and get her a chocolate protein shake and pour it into a sippy cup, she happily tries to latch on once we're on the couch. She lets out frustrated grunts as she tries but eventually I just stand and switch it to a bottle which she greedily accepts. At first she seems thrown off by the taste but soon suckles steadily. The rest of the afternoon is spent in front of the tv that's playing Disney junior, Elle even crawls to a few teething toys in her toy chest and chews after wearily looking at me to make sure it was okay. "you like your chew" I coo "ew" she says looking it and nodding. After I share some gold fish with the little one, we go to the pharmacy for my prescription. She only ate a small handful but she's opening up so much more, in the car I play soft tiny tunes. Right now some lullaby is playing, I look back to see Elle Fighting sleep while suckling her paci. She cried when

I first put her in the seat but sleep inevitably took her over, I chuckle as her eyes flutter. Once I retrieve my medicine from the pharmacy drive thou, I take it and head home, to put Eleanor down for a nap in her crib. I take Lars out to play before making some chicken and veggies for lunch.

I finish lunch when I hear the baby crying. I change her diaper and put cream all over her bum, her rash is still present but much better now. Once she's all clean I sit her in her chair and buckle her up, I try to feed her some chicken but she refused, I tried the veggies and she turns her head up at them as well. When I try another bite of chicken she lets out a scream and slams her hands down on the tray flipping her plate all over herself, I sigh as she starts wailing. I clean her the best I can but know she needs a bath, I get her some cut up fruit and lay some on her tray while I quickly eat my lunch. I put the left overs in the fridge and turn to help Ellies but see she's trying to pick up a cubed pineapple but its sliding all over the tray making her whine profusely. I chuckle before walking to her and feeding her the fruit, she does her little num num dance again; I've missed seeing it so much the last year.

Once Elle is done with her fruit I decide to give her a bottle after a bath so I lift her up and carry her to her nursery bathroom. She has lots of bath toys Im sure she will enjoy seeing again or for the first time again, I get the tub filled with warm water and put bubbles in it like I used to. She used to love the bubbles, she would pop them individually every time we took a bath together; just infatuated with them. I get her undressed and place her into the tub and help her lean against the bath pillow gently since her ribs are still broken, she looks at me scared but when I pour her many toys into the tub with her she claps and reaches for a duck. Luckily she lets me get her clean with no problem but when I turn to get her hooded towel I turn back to her leaning her face to the soapy water and slurping it up. Luckily its baby soap so its non toxic but I still get startled and rush to her before I scold her lightly "no no baby." I say lifting her from the bath, this made her sob."oh baby mommy is so sorry." I try to comfort her to no avail.

she screams the whole time I'm getting her diapered, I get her into a shirt before I turn to get changed into some sweats. Ellie is crying the whole time but seems to stop immediately when I take my shirt off, making me turn to look at her. Im taken aback when I see her just staring straight at my breasts, does she remember breastfeeding? I ask myself. When she see's me looking at her she starts whining and reaching for me, I pick her up and lay her on my lap when I sit on the bed. She stares at my nipples for a while before she slowly reaches up and lightly touches my right breast making me shiver. Im worried how she will react since I don't have milk yet, my heart stops when she mummers softly "mama" I gasp and kiss her face over and over making her push me away. "that's right I'm mama" I assure her. When she's back to her previous position she latches onto me sucking vigorously and grunting when nothing flows. She frowns around my nipple and then unlatches two minutes later with the most heart breaking shriek "milkies goed" she sobs making my heart break more, she thinks I got rid of her milk.

I stand and warm a bottle of formula with protein, once its the appropriate temperature I go back to my bed laying her across my lap once again and try to put the tip of the bottle to her lips causing her to shake her head still crying hard. She latches back onto my me so I begin to try dribbling the milk over my nipple she suckles hard when the milk touches her lip making me think my idea worked but once she has a mouth full she spits it right into my face crying and squirming around having a full meltdown. I sigh starting to get overwhelmed with the baby throwing a fit and ontop of that my chest is sticky from formula as well as my face is covered now too. I rock her until I help her latch back onto my nipple she relaxes and settles for dry nursing before she actually lets me pour more milk over my boob. She only drinks half of the eight ounce bottle but I'm just thankful she drank it, I put her paci in her mouth, before I place her blankie on her eyes like she likes. I quickly stand to wipe my chest and face before throwing a shirt on and cuddling ellie close. Ellie only takes a short nap so we eventually move to the living room and spend the rest of the afternoon playing with Ellies toys.

I feed Ellie soup for dinner which she eats all off, "my good girl eating all her num nums" I praise while cleaning our bowls, she reaches towards me "mo mo" "you want more" I ask making her nod really big. There's my little food lover, I smile to myself as I get her a baby food squeeze not wanting to upset her tummy with too much too soon. I pour her a sippy of apple juice and set it on the high chair tray, Elle mostly plays with the cup while I open her squeeze. I'm feeding Elle her pouch when my phone ring, I see its my boss and answer it, Im asked when i will be returning to work since I've been out for three days now. I decide to take off for a few weeks and explain my situation, my boss wishes me luck before he hangs up. Im happy to spend some time with my baby before I have to worry about work. I wipe Ellies face before we go to my bed, I get us both ready brushing our teeth before getting us comfy in bed. I lay a half asleep Ellie on my chest needing her as close to me as possible, I feel Lars jump onto the bed and I fall asleep with a big smile on my face.

17. Giggles and mac

A/N- hey guys I'm sorry if this chapter isn't the best, I had a hard time writing the past few days. I also want to thank everyone for reading my story! - Xx Rosie

Penelope's pov:

It's been a few days of just cuddles. Elle has gotten much better about eating her meals, she still can't finish her plate though. She hasn't been finishing her bottles either, only interested in dry nursing. Luckily while I was showering this morning I saw a few beads of milk form around my areola, I'm excited to wake my sleepy girl to try and help it flow.   I walk to her room and lift the still sleeping baby from her crib and lay her on my lap in the rocking chair, I lift my shirt and guide her parted lips to my nipple.   She suckles instantly in her sleep but once the milk starts pouring into her mouth her eyes shoot open. She unlatches with a cute gasp, "MILKIES ACK" she screams before latching on again greedily. I chuckle as she drinks hungrily. There isn't much milk causing her to whine shortly after when she runs out. I switch her to my other side before she sighs calming down. Not long after, both breasts are drained making Ellie pout with big eyes. "Aw goed?" She coos "oh baby, yes it's all gone" she hangs her head with a pout and cuddles into me. I put her on my hip to adjust my shirt, making her whine and hide her face. When I lay her on the changing table she starts to cry, I put her paci in her mouth causing her to happily suck while I get her diaper changed. When I put her in her high chair she spits her paci out happily dancing in anticipation for her oatmeal. The rest of the morning is spent nursing again, causing Ellie to nap for a few hours. She wakes up around one asking for more milkies, I nurse with her before feeding her some Mac and cheese to witch she finishes the whole bowl of. "Good job babygirl, you liked your Mac and cheese huh?" I coo at her making her nod lots "m-acmac" "that's right it's Mac baby!" I chuckle and clean her face much to her dismay. I take her to the living room and turn doc mcstuffins on for her while I tidy the house some. I'm sweeping the living room when my phone rings, I look at my phone to see it's my mom. "Hey" I answer putting the phone to my ear and hold it up with my shoulder. "We're on the way over." My mom states making me drop the broom. "Like right now?" I ask a bit panicked. I mean what If she freaks out? Ellie hasn't meet my parents yet. "Yes now." She says simply "I want to meet my grand baby and you can't keep her from us." "Mom I'm not keeping her from you, she's just been through a lot" "yes and I have lots of affection and gifts for her so let me meet her." "Ugh fine but if she freaks out then you need to leave." I say just protecting my baby. My mom chuckles "deal." I shake my head. "How far away are you?" I ask calming down some. "Pulling in now" she says before hanging up. Ugh I groan to myself, I change

Ellie's diaper and her clothes to a cute dress and pink frilly bloomers. I hear my door bell ring and Lars bark, I put Elle on my hip and head to answer the door. I open the door for my parents, as soon as Ellie sees new faces she burrows her head into my neck, hiding behind my hair. "Oh how precious!" My mother coos. I shut the door behind them and follow them to the kitchen. My parents have a seat while I make a pot of coffee, Ellie is still hiding in my hair on my hip. I bounce the girl until it's ready, I make the coffee to their liking and place them in front of them. They both thank me as I sit down and sip my own coffee when Elle tugs my shirt making me sigh. "Would you mind if I nurse her" I ask my parents wearily. They didn't like Linus when my sister found him, they thought it was some weird kink. I told them about Ellie and they were skeptical until she went missing, everything changed then. They still give Sheila and Linus the cold shoulder though and I don't find it fair. "Oh no problem, dear! The little monster needs her milkies hm?" "MILKIES?!" My baby shouts and tugs my shirt making everyone chuckle. I get her baby blanket from the living room couch and return placing it over her head before helping her latch on. She drinks happily while I catch up with my parents.

— — — — — —

After Ellie's milkies she didn't fall asleep like I had thought she would she started crawling around the house giggling up a storm. We all move to the living room and I turn on a toddler show for her making her plop her bum to the ground and grab her frog. She rubs his head across her face laying on her back staring up at the tv. I take a picture and my parents coo. Ellie is laying on our wood floor, she sticks her feet in the air and then smacks them back down. You would think this would hurt her feet. Not so. She thinks it's hysterical. She does this over and over again, after I video her cuteness I pick her up for a diaper change. Once her bum is clean I carry her back down the stairs, I put her on her play mat when my moms phone starts to ring. My baby lifts herself up by using the coffee table and balances herself before she starts bouncing her bum up and down making me giggle and dance with her. Ellie starts clapping for me which is just too stinking cute, my mom finally answers her phone after watching our moment making Elle pout. I pick her up and kiss her cheek a bunch of times "you're mommy's cutiepie" I coo making her giggle. "Alright sweetheart, we're gonna head home. I'm so glad you found your angel and you are smiling again." My dad says before kissing my head. I tell them both bye with a hug before closing the door with a sigh. Don't get me wrong I love my parents but I moved an hour away from them for a reason. Ellie starts whining in my arms, I look down at the pout on my baby's face. "Are you a hungry little monster? You want num nums?" I ask her making her nod big "num num nums" she giggles. I make chicken tortilla soup and feed Ellie, she only eats two bites before she refuses anymore getting more whiny by the second. "What's wrong babygirl" I ask before I hear a very loud toot followed by the sounds of the baby filling her diaper. "Oh my poor baby's tummy is sicky huh?" I coo making her cry harder. I bounce her as she finishes and carry her to her nursery laying her on the changing table. I clean her very messy diaper and get her into a clean one as well as a purple onesie. I get myself into comfy clothes and crawl into my bed with Ellie. Once in bed Ellie is crawling into my lap, I didn't put a shirt on so she latched on by herself. I rub her hair, "did you enjoy meeting your nonna and poppy?" I ask her making her unlach and mumble "noni an opopy" before latching back on hungrily making me smile. Such a talkative baby today, her suckles start to slow as she falls asleep. I replace my boob with her paci and put my shirt on before turning the lamp off and sliding down, pulling her closer to my body as I fall asleep myself.

18. Not your mommy

Penelope's pov:

I've been awake all night, every time I fell asleep Ellie woke me crying needing a change. Her poor belly has finally gotten better but she still refuses to sleep, She's nursed so many times my nipples are sore. I don't know how she has so much energy all of a sudden but ever since 5am she's been zooming. We had Belgian waffles this morning with cantaloupe, and Ellie devoured her whole plate before she begged for milkies. She's now sat in front of the tv watching 'Ni Hao Kai Lan,' while slamming her sippy cup on the floor when I walk in. "Ellie what are you doin?" "Mo juju" I smile "say please" "peeeeeassss" she draws out. I chuckle and get her some apple juice, when I bring it back to her she takes a sip before nodding big in approval. After a while of the baby playing and watching her show she falls asleep on her train set. I carry her to her nursery and change her diaper before putting her in her crib. I'm walking downstairs and my phone rings, when I see the caller Id my heart jumps in my chest. "Hey Candice!" I answer a bit too enthusiastically making her laugh before answering. "Hey Penny, I just left the shooting range and I'm in the neighborhood. I thought, maybe...uh...I could stop by...you know if it's no problem!" She strutters out meaning it was my turn to laugh. "I'm sure that would be no problem, I was just about to start lunch." I say making it to the kitchen and starting my plans for cucumber salad with roasted tomato and mozzarella paninis. "You're a vegetarian right?" I make sure as I start cooking. "Yeah but don't worry if you don't make anything for me." She says back quickly. "You're actually in luck, my plans are fully vegetarian!" I assure her happily. There's a few moments of silence before she speaks again "well I'm getting my guns loaded into the car now so I'll be by in about 15" she says making me internally groan at the mess. "Okay see you soon" I say before hanging up and tidying the house as quickly as possible. It takes 10 minutes for me to be satisfied with the house, I get started on the salad and put it in the fridge while I start on the first panini but get interrupted by the door bell. I walk to the door and move Lars out of the way to let Candice inside. She pets Lars as I run back to the kitchen careful to not burn my panini. I get mine plated and start on hers "everything smells so good!" She says leaning over my shoulder. I can't help but blush profusely so I lean down to let my hair cover my face. I plate her food and get the salad out plating it as well. "Would you like anything to drink?" "You have tea?" "Of course I do" I say pouring her a big glass of iced tea as well as one for me before I sit next to her to eat. "Where's the little one?" She says looking at me, I didn't realize how close she was but I can feel her breath tickle my nose. "She's uh still napping" I say having to clear my throat half way through my sentence. She smiles as she begins eating, she moans softly after her first bite, "this is amazing" she exclaims. My face is completely red at the point and after she wipes her mouth she winks at me. I go to take a bite of my own food when I hear the baby monitor erupt with cries from my girl. "Let me go get her." I say standing and hurrying up the stairs to the nursery. "There's my sleepy girl" I coo walking into the room. She sits up and reaches for me immediately. I lift her up and change her wet diaper and put her in black leggings and a big Disney princess shirt. I struggle to get socks on her feet but finally succeed and carry her downstairs. "Want to meet the lady who helped save you?" I ask her making her tilt her head at me. I walk in and she hides her face seeing Candice. "This is Candice, she helped bring you back to mommy." I say making her look at her, she points at her "C-candy? Bing 'omes?" She asks wearily making me nod "yes Candy helped bring you home." She nods and waves shyly before she looks at me "num nums?" She asks pointing to Candice's plate. "Of course baby", I say putting her in her high chair. I get her some cucumber salad and a pb&j uncrustable I had ready for her and put it on her tray making her clap and dance. She eats her bite size pieces of uncrustable and she only eats a few bites of the cucumber salad not liking the vinaigrette taste. I chuckle and kiss her head before cleaning her off "she's such a cute girl" Candice says making me turn and smile at her, "isn't she?" I get her out and put her on her play mat in the living room, she starts playing with her blocks happily. Candice and I sit on the couch for a while and talk but when she leans over and puts her arm around me Ellie toddles over and slaps Candice's knee "NO! Ot yew mommy, mines ma!" She has an angry red face and she looks at me with a pleasing look. "Oh my angel!" I coo picking her up "I am no one else's mommy, but we don't hit" I scold softly "mines mama" she says snuggling into me in full on tears. I rock her for a while before she calms down "I'm so sorry! I didn't mean to upset her" Candice explains looking worried. "Oh, no worries she's just a territorial little thing." I giggle "she'll warm up to you when she realized you aren't trying to take me away" I wink at her. She smiles back at me "I am gonna head home and get out of these sweats though. Thanks for lunch it was delicious!" She says standing. I put the baby on my hip and close the door behind her. Once she's gone my baby instantly pushes her head up my shirt. I chuckle and help her latch once I sit on the couch making her hum in happiness. Once Elle finished her milkie she just lays in my lap looking up at me while playing with my hair. I start singing Vienna by billy Joel which makes her yawn. I put her in her crib once she falls asleep and I watch an episode of a show called 'you' on Netflix. I only get an episode in before Ellie starts crying from her crib. I change the tv to Disney junior and go get my baby. I change her diaper and bring her downstairs, I sit her on her play mat while I get started on dinner. I watch Ellie try to put her toy puzzle together, I take a big breath and just smile watching my whole heart thinking hard with her tongue sticking out. No matter what happens, as long as I have this sweet angel by my side, everything's gonna be okay.

19. Weird dogs

A/N: thank you guys so much for 19k you guys are awesome!!! I've been super busy with work the last few weeks and haven't had time to post. Hopefully that will change soon. I love you all-Rosie Xx

Penelopes's pov:

Today is a very special day. Candice invited me and Ellie to the zoo, I started overthinking so I invited my sister Sheila and offered for her to bring her husband and Linus. It's not that I don't like Candice, I think I like her too much and I'm worried Ellie won't like her; especially after the hitting incident the last time she visited. The fact that she's trying so hard to get to know Elle and spend time with her as well, just makes me swoon. I thought a double date would be less stressful on Ellie. I've gotten the girl dressed in an adorable onesie with bunnies and white tutu, she looks so precious I can't stop cooing at her. She's been dressed for 30 minutes now and we're eating breakfast in the kitchen waiting for everyone to arrive. "Aren't you just the cutest baby today?" I coo again tickling her shoeless feet. I packed her shoes in her diaper bag cause she always kicks them off in the car. This will be Ellie's longest car ride since the zoo is basically an hour away, she normally cries until she falls asleep. I warned everyone of Ellie's fear of cars but they all want to ride in my suv. I feed Ellie her oatmeal until she refuses more and lay her across my lap. Before I have a chance to pull my shirt down Ellie is yelling "milkies" at the top of her lungs. she finally takes a breath when my shirt comes off, her red face returns to her natural color before she latches on hungrily. I chuckle and play with her hair while she drinks her milk, I've tried watching tv and playing a game on my phone but Ellie likes all attention on her during milkie time. 5 minutes after my shirt is pulled down I start getting "I'm here" texts. Ellie is asleep so I lift her gently in my arms, when I open the door I put my finger to my mouth to indicate Ellie is sleeping. They all nod knowing Ellie's car fear. We all hope she sleeps the whole time, once she's strapped in, shiela's husband places a still sleepy Linus next to Ellie before getting all the way in the back seat next to my sister as I start to play quick lullabies for the little ones. Once candice is in the passenger seat I start our journey.

• • • • • Luckily Elle and Linus sleep the whole ride, I stopped and get us all coffees making me have to pee horrendously. My leg is jiggling as I lean over and whisper to Candice "hey, gotta pee, don't wake the babies till I get back!" I say quickly as I rush to the bathrooms near the entrance. It takes me a while to empty my bladder fully, as soon as I open the bathroom door I hear a babies cries. Not just any baby, my baby, I run to the car and grab my sobbing child from my sisters arms as she was trying so desperately to sooth my distraught daughter. "I-I'm sorry she woke up and was looking for you, I-I told her you'd be right back but she wouldn't listen she just keep screaming give me my mommy back" my sister says In a panic. I nod as I rock Ellie, her grip my my shirt is tight and slightly painful as she has a fist of my hair but I don't care. "Hey hey, sweet baby. Mommy would never leave you" I try to sooth her. After a few minutes of sniffles and then a few more minutes of milk. I look down as I hold the bottle for her, she's looking up at me with the saddest eyes. It took a lot of convincing to get Ellie to take the bottle but eventually she gave in. Elle spits the nipple out of her mouth half way through her bottle "m-a ilkies, mama peas" my baby sniffles as she lays a soft hand on my left breast. I sigh sadly "when we get home baby I promise." I say putting my hand over hers but my words cause her to erupt in more sobs and she tries to wiggle out of my hold. She cries for another 5 minutes until I finally get her to notice the animal pictures on the wall of the ticket office. She continues to cry silently as she looks around. "Oggies?" She asks looking at me with big eyes, I wipe her tears and without thinking I nod my head making her clap and jump up and down on my hip. I look up and it's then I realize I did something wrong, there's no dogs at the zoo. We all get out and get the babies in their strollers before we get our tickets. We decided to go to the birds first, I giggle at my babies oos and ahhs from her stroller. There's nothing better than seeing the delight of a little one seeing something for the first time, I smile at my baby trying to soak this up when I feel a hand on my arm. "I'm really glad you came" the words are so soft the tickle my ear and by the time I register what was said she's already back to telling Linus all about her job. "So you are like a hero?" I hear him ask her making me chuckle. "Oggies" Elle shouts pointing at a parrot making everyone laugh. "I knew that would backfire on you" I hear Astian say between breaths. I playfully roll my eyes, unfortunately no matter how we tell Ellie that the other animals aren't dogs; she just doesn't grasp it. She does end up with a turtle stuffed animal from Sheila and a red panda from me which are both her new doggies. As we are leaving the gift shop Elle gaps and grabs a deer stuffy "Oggies ooooooooo" she says mesmerized. "Baby mommy got you a stuffie" I tell her softly. She pouts but before the tears have a chance to fall I hear Candice tell the cashier to ring her up for the deer stuffie. I sigh but smile at her especially when I hear my little one shout a thank you and hug her from her stroller "fank yew candy" she says again. We all get loaded into the car after a nice lunch in the zoo cafe and the baby gets a diaper change. The moment Elle leaves my arms and I start strapping her in she starts thrashing in her seat. I struggle to get her buckled and kiss her head before I close her door. "Ma noooo peasss" I hear as I circle the car and get into the drivers seat. We all sing to her and take turns trying different tactics to calm her down but nothing works. The whole hour the car is filled with screams and sobs, she starts to slow her sobs as I pull into the driveway, finally tiring herself out. She's sniffling and wheezing, I wave bye to everyone as they load into their own cars. Once we get into the house I lift my shirt and sure enough she latched in and gulps it down like it's going to disappear. Slow down, bug" I coo she huffs but slows her suckles just a little. I smile at her as her eyes get heavy. "You had a long day huh?" I say rubbing her back soothingly "you're mommy's sleepy girl" I coo as she drifts off. I start humming and within minutes she's asleep, I hold her in my arms as I watch tv on the couch; enjoying Lars snuggles and Ellie's warmth. I take Elle to her crib and go to bed, I fall asleep thinking of the day and how loved I feel.

20. New people

Today is the day...

It's finally here...

I'm holding Elle in my arms as we stand in a judges office with the adoption papers right in front of us. I sign them while crying knowing now I can go to any lengths to protect my girl. I walk out of the building and sit in the back to nurse Elle, she falls asleep with her blanket covering her eyes. I detach her from my nipple and replace it with her paci, I'm the drive home I order myself and Candice a cold brew since she's meeting me at the house awaiting the good news. I decide to treat Ellie and get her two spinkled donuts, I try to avoid sugary things but she deserves to indulge in life's little delights. I place the sleeping child in her crib to nap, and sit at the kitchen table with my sketch book. I hear the doorbell ring 29 minutes later, I skip to the door and open it wide. "She's my daughter" I whisper shout. She smiles and grabs me up spinning me in a circle, "I'm so so happy for you both" she says only a few inches from my face. I blush and step back into the house tucking a strand of hair behind my ear and looking down. "I got you your coffee" I say shyly pointing into the kitchen as I close the door. "It's in the table" I say following her to the kitchen. She takes a sip "perfect" she exclaims as if I made it myself. I smile and take a sip of my own. "I'm so ecstatic I invite; Mel, my parents, brother, as well as Shiela and Linus over for dinner, will you please come?" I ask her with a wide grin. "I'd be delighted" she responds and leans forward, I lean in as well and look down before meeting her gaze again, my heart rate quickens just as the baby monitor lets loose the sounds of a unhappy baby. I look over at the monitor and back at her, I stand but pause before I hear a blood curdling scream from Elle causing me to run to her nursery. "Mama? MAMAAAAAA" I hear as I walk into her room. "Hush now my love, you're safe" I try to comfort. She reaches for me and I notice she's wet, I lift her and get her undressed out of her pee and sweat soaked clothes. "Did my poor angel have a bad dream?" I ask in realization. In that moment the baby let's her bowels loose all over the changing table and me causing a squeal to escape from me. In the panic I let go of the baby causing her to drop the inch she was above the table and land on it lightly; regardless of the small impact she still lets out the most heartbreaking sob. As I try to figure out what to do Candice walks in. "I uh heard on the monitor" she explains ans then makes a cringe face before she softens with a look of sympathy. "Let's get you two cleaned up" Candice says. All I can do is nod as she lifts the baby not even caring about her clothes and then lightly leads me to my bathroom. "Step in" she instructs me and points to the tub. I step in and she gets the spray nozzle ready. Ellie is still crying softly but watching intently to the scene while holding tightly to Candy's hair.

"Would you be uncomfortable to get undressed in front of me" she asks. I think and decide at this point there's nothing, not even being nude in front of the girl I have a thing for the first time, that can keep me in these clothes. I get undressed as she adjusts the temperature making sure it's not too hot or cold and sprays me off. "You know I can do this" I say a little more coherent now. She chuckled and just keeps spraying me, once I'm clean she undressed the baby gently and hands her to me. I take her softly and smile sadly down at her. "My angel doesn't feel well huh?" I ask making her rub her face into my chest but not for milk which answers my question. I look up at Candice and she smile softly before going to spray Ellie too. Once we are done we get out and get dressed while candy gets in the shower. I leave her a pair of clothes and order food for the guest that will arrive in a few hours. I make us some chicken wraps and sweet potato fries for lunch, Ellie doesn't like it much but eats the chicken out if it. After our lunch Candice show Elle her favorite Disney movie. I watch Elle enjoy her first Disney movie, zootopia. "Bun Ike yew" my baby coos, after the movie Candice give Elle a surprise she had for her. It's a dog coloring book with a pack of crayons, I watch Elle's confused face. "Wat dat" she says and watches Candice open the book to a page and start to color in the dog making Elle gasp in amazement. "Ama ook! Candy ake colors!!" I giggle "candy is making colors" i walk over "why don't you try, lovely?" I offer her an orange crayon making her smile wide. I watch Candice and Elle color until my family arrives. We all have a wonderful dinner, Elle hide in my chest the whole time and refused to acknowledge anyone except me,

Mel, and Candice. I told everyone we will have to try one on one and they all understood. Once everyone left I told Ellie she could have her donuts. "Wat dooo-nut ma-ma?" My baby says innocently. I smile and get her donuts during them into small bites and I give her a few bites of each not wanting her to have a whole donuts worth. She eat the vanilla with sprinkles first and her eyes widen "is it yummy sweet girl?" I ask making her nod big. Then she tries the chocolate frosted making her ignore the rest of her vanilla, she eats the chocolate quickly and then pouts. There's 3 bite size pieces of a vanilla frosted donut on her high chair. "Mama" I see my baby struggling to Ask for the chocolate without knowing how. "Otter doo-nut" "other donut?" I question as I get 3 bite size peices of the chocolate and put it in her tray making her nod. "Fankies my mama" she says kindly before getting more frosting in her face then in her belly. I clean her up and get her diaper changed, let's get those teethies brushes" I say helping her brush. Once we're both ready for bed I go to sit in the rocking chair like I usually do by Ellie whines. "What is it babygirl?" "Eep ma, peas eep ma" I sigh knowing she's still scared to sleep. "Of course angel" I say kissing her head. I feel her body relax and I tear up as I cover us up underneath the blankets. "Mommy loves you more than anything in this world, you are my daughter, my baby, forever I will care for you."

21. My Superhero

I woke up at 5am this morning to Elle bouncing her bum on my tummy asking for breakfast. I made us pancakes and we watched more Disney movies per her request. I've noticed Elle has become a bit bored of her toys, she still plays with them but not with the same excitement so I'm going to surprise her with a trip to the toy shop. I text Candice and tell her we're going to the mall and invite her, a few minutes later while Ellie is nursing she respond saying she'd love too. She gets off work at 12pm so we decided to meet at 1:30. I get Ellie dressed and make us lunch, just a simple nuggets and fries. >> • • << Candice, Elle, and I arrive at the mall, I get Ellie situated in her stroller; she's still asleep from after nursing before Candice arrived. I push Ellie into the mall with Candice right beside me. "Where to first? I can't really get Ellie toys until she's awake" I chuckle and look over at her. "Let's get a coffee and then just window shop till little cutie wakes up." I happily nod in response. Once Elle wakes up I take her to the bathroom for a diaper change. I carry her out and Candice offers to push the empty stroller, we walk to the toy store making Elle peak out from my hair she has draped over her like a curtain. I giggle, "let's get this little one some new thinga ma bobs" I exclaim making her squeal happily and giggle. She's picks out toys in my arms shyly until she sees a dollhouse causing her to gasp, wiggle and squirms till I put her on her feet; she's still a little unsteady on her feet so I try to hold her hands but she is too excited and runs towards it falling into it giggling. "Alright baby let's be careful alright?" I say to her softly before I let her pick out the dollhouse she wants and when I turn to put it in our cart she's gone by the time I turn around. "Elle?" I ask looking around, I check the neighboring aisles while my heart beat starts jumping out of my chest.

"ELLE? Ellie? Please oh god ELEANOR!?!!" I scream. Candice takes off running past me making me start to scream for her as well but stop when I see her look around confused, "what's going on?" She doesn't answer and runs into a nearby store. I follow her as she looks all over until she stops in front of a dressing room. She kicks the door down and there stands a man holding my daughter in his nasty hands. I scream and kick him in between the legs knocking him to the ground and take my child from his arms before Candice handcuffs him. She hold him until the cops on duty can take him away. Eleanor is silently staring up at the ceiling making my heart sink. My poor baby is so scared she can't even cry, I tear up but push it away for later, she needs me. I send Candice to the store to buy Ellie her toys and I take her to the car. "Babygirl don't ever let go of mommy's hand in public ever again" I say sternly as Candice gets back into the car. "Hey she doesn't understand, and your tone is scaring her!" She says "she just experienced more trauma after a traumatizing life and this could make her think that she did something wrong for enjoying herself and she's always going to be on guard." I pause and look down at Elle, she has big wide doe eyes and she does look scared of me. I start crying and I pull her close to me holding onto her "mommy didn't mean to scare you, And I know you don't understand me fully but I just don't want to lose you again" I sob into her hair for a moment before I kiss her head and wipe my tears away. Elle grabs my shirt and just stars at me with her big eyes making my heartache. Once home I try to get Elle to nurse and she refuses. She won't look at her new or old toys. All she accepts is her blankie, I sigh when she does take the cloth from my hand and take it as a win before I stand with her in my arms. I make us all a pizza while Ellie sits in her playpen. I put her new toys in there for her but she just lays on her blanket with her paci in her mouth, I turn on Disney junior for her making her hum somewhat. Elle refuses to eat making me frown since she doesn't want mommy milk either. The whole next hour I spend trying to feed her to no avail, "Ellie please eat for mama?" I please but all she does is lay her head down onto the pizza slice. I cringe and slip the pizza out from under her before cleaning her face with no fight. I get a jar of baby food and try a few times before she does take a few bites. She only takes 3 bites but it's all she's accepted all day making me relived somewhat. "Come on baby let's go to bed" I say lifting her up and carrying her to bed. I get her diaper changed and put her in a soft onesie before laying her on my chest. I take my shirt off and try to nurse one last time only to get rejected once more.

I leave my shirt off for the night just in case she changes her mind. I drift off to sleep only after I'm sure Elle is down for the night.

22. Grandparents

I wake up at 7 in the morning to Elle wide awake staring at the ceiling. "Hey babygirl" I coo but she doesn't move, I feel her diaper and sigh. "Let's get you changed for the day, princess" I say softly and get myself ready once she's in her soft sweater and shorts. I left my shirt off to try to convince Elle to nurse, I'm so full if she doesn't I'll have to pump; I internally groan at the idea. Droplets of milk are beading off my nipples as I sit against my made bed bringing the small girl to my lap. I try dragging my nipple across her lips but she just turns her head with her lips pressed tightly together. "Drink your milkies for mama" I beg her but she just stars back at me with sad eyes. I give up for now and take her to the playpen in the living room. I get my pump ready and sit on the couch, once my breasts are emptied. I go to the kitchen to get us some breakfast made. I make Elle some oatmeal and myself a bagel with strawberry cream cheese. I pick Elle up from the same position I sat her in. I sit her in her high chair, I then give her a frozen strawberry in a teething toy while I eat my bagel; hoping it will increase her appetite some. Once I'm halfway through my breakfast she puts her teether down and reaches forward to try and grab my bagel. She doesn't get it from my hand but when she lets go her hand is covered in cream cheese which she licks off with only a moment of hesitation. I smile and give her the last small bite of my bagel and get her cooled off oatmeal. After she eats about 1/4 of the bowl, I congratulate her over and over. "Mama is so proud of you." I say making her smile slightly. I gasp, "I missed that darling smile" I coo as I clean her hands and face. This time when I lift her up she clings to the front of my body making all the tension melt from my body. I let out all the tears I was holding in and hold her tightly to me as I walk us to the living room, abandoning our dishes. I turn on a random Disney movie and rock her. She doesn't look at the tv, just me, she reaches towards me slowly and rests her little palm to my cheek. "I love you, my angel" I tell her making her giggle "wuv mama!" The rest of our morning is spent like this, with movies playing in the background as we hold each other. Elle is still refusing to eat much for some reason though, and she won't let me place her down without having a fit. As Elle and I are playing with her dollies, my mom calls me. I answer making Elle look up at me from my lap not liking that my attention has been taken away from her. I smile and hold her closer to me in hops it will calm her, she relaxes some and I hand her her paci causing her to lean into me and watch me closely as I talk to my mother. "Hi mom""Darling, how is our grand baby?" I look down at Ellie playing with her feet. "She's doing better, very much opening back up" "oh good we're coming over" I sigh "mom you know she gets scared easily. "And we just want to see you both l, we won't do anything to make her unhappy" my mom kinda pleads. I agree and get Elle into a new diaper, when I lay her on the changing table she loses it. She's reaching for me and screaming her little head off, even trying to roll off the table. I struggle to get her changed and back into my arms but once I do she calms immediately. "What am I gonna do with you" I whisper and get the bottle I pumped earlier out of the fridge and try to get her to latch on she starts to suckle but spits it out. I realize she probably doesn't like the cold so I warm it for her and try again, this time she sucks half the bottle down before spitting it out and burping. I wipe her face lift her up kissing her little face. It's then the doorbell rings making Elle cling to me again with big eyes. "Hey it's okay babygirl" I coo while standing up with her. I open the door and she hides from my parents as I greet them. After about 30 minutes we're all sat at the kitchen table. My dad with black cup of coffee and my mom with a cup light and sweet like mine. Elle has not moved from her spot attached to my chest while we chat. My mom eventually gets her book out and my dad gets a puzzle out and starts putting it together at the table but this does get Elle's attention. She watches intently as her 'op-op' puts it together. We all have five cheese ziti and Elle eats a few handfuls before she refuses. After dinner I sing her Vienna by Billie Joel. "Sing it gain mama" my baby claps. I end up singing the song 6 or 7 times before I try to say no but it causes my baby to erupt in tears. "Gain gain gain" Ellie bawls. I keep singing but finally get her to latch onto my nipple, her eyes start to get heavy the 12th time I sing the song. Once Elle is asleep my parents say their goodbyes, I lock them out and go to place Ellie in her crib. My phone rings as I'm getting ready for bed "hey Candice" I greet happily. "Hey there, how was your day?" We talk for sometime before it gets a little late. "Hey so I wanted to ask this in person but I can't seem to wait." Candice says. "What's up?" I get curious and sit up in my bed. "Would you be my girlfriend?" Her question throws me off. I pause for a moment and think of Ellie, worried it will throw her back into hiding. "If it's too early..." I cut her off realizing this is about how I feel and how Candice feels...

"Of course I will be your girlfriend."

23. Mommy blue's

Candice is mine, I can't believe it. I just don't know how to explain it to Ellie, that thought goes through my mind when I hear cries over the baby monitor. I get out of bed and hurry to my babygirl, upon opening the door the first thing I see is her little body holding herself up in the bars of her crib. "Ma" my baby sobs. "Mama is here baby" I coo while lifting her up and cuddle her close as I carry her to the changing table "let's get you out of this nasty diapey, hm?" I try to calm her tears but she keeps sobbing until I pick her back up and she begs for milkies. I sit down quickly in the rocking chair and lift my shirt up, I rarely wear bras anymore. I help my little one latch, her sobs turn to hums. My phone vibrates pulling my attention away from my darling babygirl, I shift slightly and pull my phone my pocket trying not to disturb Elle. I see that it's my boss and I take a breath in to prepare to speak professionally. "Hello Sir, how are you?" I greet immediately. "Good morning Penelope, I'm well. How are you and Miss. Ellie doing?" My boss asks nicely. We chat for a moment before we get to the reason for calling. "I'm sorry to disturb you so early but I've had some issues at the office. Is there anyway you can come down?" I cringe at the thought of leaving my baby but I've never heard my boss plead before. "Let me see if I can find a babysitter." I say. "Thank you so much, you're the best Penny" I smile and hang up before calling my parents, unfortunately they are both in the next state away at a flee market. My only other option is to see if Candice is off today. If she is I'm going to have to ask her to sit with me and Elle when I get back and explain what it means for us to be together and make sure Elle is okay with that. I smile down at my girl who unlatches to smile at me, I wipe her face and lift her up getting her dressed before I call Candice. "Hello" "hey there" "hey" "hi" she says tiredly making me giggle. "Good morning sleepy head" she just groans. "Well I'm sorry to bother you but my boss asked me to come into the office and My parents aren't in town-" "I'd love to watch that sweet angel" Candice cuts me off not sounding tired anymore. I can't help but smile at the idea she was excited enough to fully wake up. "I'll get ready and be on my way" "thank you so much, I owe you one." "No way I'm so excited to hang out with little Ellie today, I'll see you soon" and with that she hung up. I get dressed as quickly as possible and feed Ellie some pancakes. By the time I'm cleaning her up the doorbell rings letting me know Candice is here. I let her in and greet her with a hug. "Candy" my baby says with a wave making Candice smile and kiss her head. "Hi there Ellie bug" she coos. I look down and realize I need to get dressed still and frown. "Can you watch her while I get dressed? If she cries you can come sit with me" I say and she nods before carrying my sweet baby to the couch. I rush upstairs and get dressed as quickly as I can into a pencil skirt and blouse with a bow on the front. I go into my bathroom and start on my hair and makeup when my door opens. I turn and smile at Candice and Elle. "We missed you" Candice says sheepishly and Ellie backs her up "miss chu!" She yells. "I missed you both" I say and wink at Candice before going back to my makeup. I watch Candice and Elle dance to the music I have playing, it's not the most appropriate music for her age but she doesn't understand so I leave it on for now. When my makeup is done I walk to Ellie and lift her up, the first thing she does is try to untie the bow on my blouse. I pull her hand away and kiss her head. "I'll get this little one dressed for the day. She's already had breakfast and milk but will probably want a bottle before lunch time. I can leave some cash on the table for take out since I didn't have time to prepare anything for you both." I explain finishing up my makeup. "Oh no it's my treat for the little one don't worry" she protests and before I have a chance to argue she says "please" I nod and walk into the nursery with them following closely behind. Candice puts Ellie down and she crawls to her toy box. "Ellie I gotta get you dressed sweet pea" I coo she grabs a stuffed banana and crawls to me. I smile and find her a yellow onesie and jean shorts with bananas on it to match her stuffed friend. "Ma nana" she points as I get her changed into a fresh diaper and her outfit. "That's right angel" I coo as I get her socks on her little feet. Candice comes and picks up my little one, i tear up at the thought of leaving her for the day. Candice leans in and kisses my cheek before whispering "don't worry I'll take good care of her and we will have lots of fun" i smile and realize I'm running late. "Okay bug, mama has to go to work for the day, be good for Candy" "w-oke?" My baby tilts her head "don't worry mama will be back" I kiss her head and run out the door before the waterworks start.

Candice's pov:

The day has gone so smoothly we watch Disney junior and I took Ellie to the park, I got her a happy meal and by the time we arrive home and I get her out of the car seat Penny left in the garage she's pulling back into the driveway. "MAMA" she screams and toddles off towards Penny who picks her up and spins her around. "How'd she do?" "Amazing only cried for a bout 30 minutes" i say and explain what we did for the rest of the day "marvelous, mommy is so proud of you angel" she says as Ellie reaches her hand down her blouse. Penny giggles "would you like to stay for dinner" i nod and wonder if we're gonna tell Ellie of our relationship.

24. Two birthday's

A/n: I'm sorry I've had such bad writers block and I know this chapter isn't the best but I have a lot of ideas for the other half of this story so try to bare with me. Thank you for reading. -Rosie

Candice and I talked to Ellie about our relationship, she didn't fully understand what it meant. "Dis mean Candy pay wid me mo?" Is all she asked. Candice said said of course making Elle nod happily. Today Candice and I are planning a party for Ellie. The doctor said Ellie aged mentally even apart from me making her headspace 2 years old. I've decided she missed out on too many birthdays, so we Will celebrate her gotcha day which was 2 years ago today when I found her in the mall; and the day she was born. I invited my family and decorated the house while Elle was down for her morning nap. Candice picked up the cake and I made a charcuterie board and tacos for everyone. I hear coos coming from the baby monitor, when I walk into Ellie's room I see her laying down playing with her frog. "Good morning lovebug" I coo pulling the bar down. She smiles when I lift her up "my mama" she snuggles into me. I sit in the rocking chair and breast feed her. Once she's done I get her dressed into her birthday outfit. It's 11:30 and the guest will be here in 30 minutes. I make birthday pancakes for Ellie and tell her about her special day. "Today is the day mama found you and we are gonna celebrate you coming home with me" "love mama" she pats her high chair tray. "I love you babygirl." The doorbell rings, I answer the door revealing Candice. After a kiss on the cheek we walk into the living room, "it looks so cute in here" Candice coos at the pink decorations. When we walk into the kitchen Ellie is covered in pink frosting and smiling at us "candy candy" she reaches with grabby hands. "Let mama clean you off, bug" I chuckle and wipe her clean before handing her to Candice. She snuggles into her while we go back into the living room, I turn on Minnie Mouse while we wait for the guests to arrive. • • • • •• • • • •• • • • • •• • • • • Everyone is here and eating, Ellie is surprisingly hyper she tells everyone it's her "got got day" making everyone laugh. After everyone is finished eating it's time for the cake, I pick Ellie up and Candice brings the cake over and lights the candles we all start singing happy birthday making her clap excitedly. I help her blow the candles out and Candice cuts the cake. I put Ellie in her high chair and put a bib in her before we hand her her first cake ever. We video her shove the whole thing in her mouth. We all have a piece of cake before I clean her off and go to the living room for gifts. Candice and I sit and help her open all her gifts. She gots lots of stuffies and puzzles. We also got her coloring supplies "ook ama oggiss" she says pointing at one of the coloring books. "That's right baby!" Once all the gifts are open I turn the tv to cartoons while she plays with her new blocks. I make us coffee while Linus and Ellie play, after about an hour Ellie crawls to me on the couch. I set my coffee cup down and lift her up, "you enjoying your new toys love?" She nods big and pats my boob I smile and tell everyone I'll be back. I take her upstairs and sit in her rocking chair, I lift my shirt up and she latches on fast. I rub her hair "you're a hungry little one hm?" I ask making her grunt. Candice come into the room and sits on the floor "hi pretty lady" i great her making her smile. "Your family said to tell you they're gonna head out when Ellie is finished." I smile "that's good this little one will want a nap soon" i say making her nod "me too" she giggles "we could have a nap together?" I suggest shyly "I'd like that very much" she says when I stand to change Ellie's diaper. We walk out together and tell everyone bye Ellie waves sleepily. We sit on the couch with Ellie while she watches the cartoon. 10 minutes in and she's asleep, I take her to her crib and lead candice to my room. "Here's some sleep pants you can wear if you'd like" i say opening my drawer and handing them over she thanks me and goes into the bathroom while I change into some shorts. We cuddle up under the covers when she returns. "I had a good time today" she says sleepily. "I did too, having you by my side definitely brightens up any occasion even with my parents involved" I chuckle "they mean well" she smiles making me nod. She kisses my head and I drift to sleep. When we wake up I decide to make dinner, I make a veggie pasta and head to wake Ellie up when it's done. I change her diaper and bring her to the kitchen. She eats it all making a big mess. I clean her up and I nurse her on the couch. Candice stayed and watched a movie with us before she went home.

Ellie fell asleep in my arms shortly after, I put her in her crib and go to bed, happy with how the day turned out.

25. Lets meet Miss. May

I woke up extra early today, my boss wants me to see clients in the office more which would mean I need someone to watch Ellie. I've done a lot of research and considering Ellie's case I'd like her to have an education. I found this age regression daycare nearby, I gave them a call and they are extremely willing to support Ellie's case. I even went and met the teacher Miss. May, She was so kind and accepting of Ellie's situation. I'm just worried how Elle is gonna react, in the long run I believe this will be good for her. I get all of Ellie's school supplies I bought packed into her new backpack and put all her diapers and necessities into her diaper bag. I wake my munchkin up and we spend some time nursing before I get her dressed into some pink overalls and a sweater for the day. "Don't you look adorable" i praise "where goin mama?" I smile and put her in my hip. "Well we're going to a place called sunny Springs, they have lots of toys and coloring books" i tell her excitedly "reawwy ama?" She bounces on my hit. "Yes baby" I kiss her head and put her in her hair chair before I feed her the oatmeal I made before I woke her. She finishes pretty quickly, I wake her off and I carry her to the car. I play tiny tunes until we pull up. I take a deep breath and walk around to pick my baby up. I walk inside and sign her in before I walk into Miss. May's classroom. Miss. May greets Ellie making her hide in my hair. She takes her bags and shows me her cubby, we show Ellie the toy area where she does crawl down and play with some blocks. I talk with Miss. may before she tells me it's best to not say goodbye but to sneak out while they're distracted but the thought breaks my heart so kneel down. "Hi ama" "hi baby, mama needs to go to work but I will be back I promise" I assure her but she shakes her head and clings to me "nu ama nu eeve" I tear up and kiss her head before I pull her off me lightly. "Peas Ama nuu" Ellie wails when miss May picks her up. I walk out of the door but stand outside and listen as miss may tries to soothe her i peep in and see Ellie has hidden under the farthest desk closest to the wall making me break down and cry when some other parents show up to drop off their kids. I walk to my car and drive to work knowing she will call if she doesn't calm down. By lunchtime I'm surprised I haven't been called, I eat half my lunch when I see her name pop up in the screen. I answer it quickly. "Hello" "I'm so sorry to bother you penny but Ellie is so distraught and kicks and screams if anyone tries to touch or move her. I think she's had enough for today" "thank you May I appreciate the call I'm on the way. I hang up and tell my boss, he says he'll cancel my appointments for me. I thank him and run out of the door, once I make it to the school I rush inside and to the classroom. When I open the door I see Ellie in the same spot I saw her crawl into when I left. My heart sinks and I walk over to her, she doesn't see me at first, "lovebug?" "Ama!" She screams and jumps into my arms "I told you I'd be back babygirl" she nods and squeezes me tightly I wave at the teacher and carry her to the car buckling her into her car seat. I give her one of the bottles I left at the daycare for her since she clearly didn't eat. She drinks it quickly but falls asleep before she finishes. I sit in the car with her for a little bit before I lift her up and take her to her crib. I change my clothes and lay down pretty tired from the day and worry. I'm woken up by my baby's cries. I rush to her crib and pick her up lifting my shirt up and sitting in the rocking chair letting her drink her milkies. She finishes with a burp and a giggle. I smile and kiss her little nose. I carry her to her play pen and turn on bubble guppies for her while I cook. Once done with the veggie soup I put her in her high chair and slowly feed her as I eat, she finishes all her food. I clean her up and place her down. She crawls to gets a coloring book and crayons and sits on her play mat, I smile and sit with her and color the other page. She starts to fall asleep on the book so I lift her up and clean up the crayons so Lars doesn't eat them and carry her to her crib for the night. I have a hard time falling asleep so I call Candice. We talk for a few hours before I start to get sleepy but I don't want to hang up so I let myself fall asleep on the phone listening to her melodic voice.

26. Better days

A/N- so I noticed my book has been added to a few smut readings lists and this is a completely sfw book. Please do not add this to book to nsfw lists. Thank you.

Ellie has gotten used to daycare and even waves buh bye now and blows kisses. She doesn't interact with any of the kids though and will only sit with her teacher. I'm happy she doesn't hate school and likes her teacher but I wish she would try to play with her classmates. She got up excited to play with Miss. May every morning this week including today which is Saturday. "Babygirl it's the weekend, which means you stay with mommy today and tomorrow. She smiles and snuggles into my shoulder, "day wiff mama!!" I chuckle and carry Ellie down to have breakfast once she finishes her milk. Ellie eats all her breakfast when I decide to call Candice but she doesn't answer making me remember she had work today. She's been working a lot on this case and I haven't heard from her much. Ellie and I spend the day watching tv and movies for a few hours before she falls asleep laying on top of me.A few hours into Ellie's nap Candice calls me back. "Hey there gorgeous" I greet my girlfriend. She chuckled before replying "I'm sorry I missed your call I've been caught up in this case. But I'm gonna be off in an hour, is there anyway I can take you out last minute? I want to take you on a date but I'll be busy with work the next few weeks" she rambles before sighing. I think for a moment before telling her I should call my parents or sister to see if anyone is free. "Alright love, let me know" "I will, talk later" I hang up and dial my moms number. "Hi angel!" My moms excited tone rings in my ears. "Hi mom, I'm sorry if it's short notice but can you watch Elle tonight?""Oh finally I get to babysit the little one?" She asks in a high pitch voice. I pull the phone from my ear some and sigh at the idea of leaving Elle for the first time. "Yes, Candice is taking me out. I'll text you the details?" "Okay love" we say our goodbyes before I hang up the phone. I look down at Ellie and pull her close to me, she says I'll at my shirt and I help her latch on while I worry about Ellie thinking I won't come back tonight. After the trauma she endured when she got taken I haven't even though of leaving her with a babysitter, but I know I can't always bring her with me and it's a good learning opportunity for Elle to realize that her mommy will come back. I sigh and switch Ellie to the other boob going to my phone to text Candice about the details. I have 4 hours to get Ellie down for a nap, make some lunch, and get myself ready. I look down to realize Ellie is already asleep, well that's one thing taken care of. I drop Ellie off in her crib Turing the baby monitor on and heading to the kitchen to make myself a sandwich and a side of fruit. I decide to eat in front of the tv so I turn on bobs burgers, liking the break from all the baby cartoons I watch with Ellie. I finish my lunch and think to myself that I should shower while the baby is asleep. I turn the water on and hope in, listening to some music while I clean myself. I'm half way through my makeup routine when I hear Ellie's soft cries through the monitor. I walk to the nursery and pick my baby up. "Did you have a good nap baby?" My little one nods and snuggles into my shoulder. I lay her on the changing table and change her diaper quickly while she fusses and move her to the rocking chair to nurse. My baby latches on and suckles fast while I rock her. I look at the time and realize my mom will be here any moment and I need to finish getting ready. Once Ellie unlatches I carry her to my bathroom and set her on a baby play mat I have on the floor before I hand her a few toys from her toy box in my room I have for this reason. I return to my makeup and put my hair into a braided bun and get dressed in a flowery high low dress and combat boots. Once I finish I hear my doorbell ring, I pick Ellie up "mama had a surprise for you lovebug" "a prise?" "Mhmm that's right baby" I open the door to reveal my mother making Ellie reach out with grabby hands "NONI" my baby screams, and I hand her over. We sit on the couch and wait for Candice to arrive, after 10 minutes of catching up and bubble guppies we hear a knock on the door. "Prise?" My baby asks adorably. I giggle and pick her up, "let's see who's at the door hm?" My baby bounces excitedly while I open the door "candyyyyyyy" Ellie sing songs reaching for her, once again I hand her over and give Candice a kiss in the check which Ellie covers with her own kiss making us both chuckle. "Reservations are in 30 minutes, you ready?" I nod slightly and take Ellie giving her a kiss on the head. "You're gonna play with Noni for a little bit okay baby" "mama aye oo?" Ellie asks with a tilt of her head. Candice and I share a look before I reply "when mama gets back we will all play before Noni leaves how about that?" "Ma nu go" my baby sniffles and lays her head on my shoulder. I kiss her head and hand her to my mom, she takes her over to her toys and starts to distract her. Candice and I manage to sneak out but before we make it to the car we hear Ellie's sobs come from the house. We share a sad look and get in the car, the ride is silent aside from the soft music coming from the speaker. I can't stop thinking about how sad Ellie must be, I look up when we pull into the parking spot. Candice gets out and opens my door for me taking my hand leading me to the door of the restaurant. I open the door for her and we walk in. Candice handles the reservations and we are lead to our table. ••• After we finish dinner Candice takes me for a walk around the block. "I was going to take you to that little ice cream shop, but I can't stop thinking about Ellie and I see on your face you can't either." She pauses for a moment "let's go be with our girl hm?" I smile up at her brightly, she called Ellie our girl. My heart feels like it's about to burst out of my chest when she starts to lean down, I look into her eyes before they close as our lips met. ••• We make it to my house and walk into my mom and my baby watching finding Nemo. We share a look and plop onto the couch next to them "mommy! Candy!" Ellie climbs onto my lap and gives me a big kiss before reaching for Candice to do the same. We finish the movie before my mom tells us bye and leaves before it gets too late. Candice and I are coloring with Ellie when she gets a call, she stands to go into the kitchen. I frown but go back to the coloring page, when she returns she crouches down next to me. "I need to go to work, I'm sorry I can't stay and color with you beautiful lady's" she tells us before kissing my nose and then Ellie's. "I'll see you soon" she says and stands to grab her bag, waving at Ellie and blowing me a kiss before exiting the house. "Candy goed" my baby pouts pulling herself into my lap and tugging my shirt as she sniffles. "I miss candy too baby" I kiss her head and get her ready to nurse. We sit like that till my baby falls asleep, I carry her to my room and get undressed before crawling into bed with my little one, I close my eyes and drift off to sleep wishing Candice was here with us.

CPSIA information can be obtained
at www.ICGtesting.com
Printed in the USA
LVHW080549280223
740519LV00015B/259